By Erle Stanley Gardner
Published by Ballantine Books:

The Case of the
Careless Cupid

Erle Stanley Gardner

BALLANTINE BOOKS • NEW YORK

Copyright © 1968 by Erle Stanley Gardner

All rights reserved under International and Pan-American Copyright Conventions. Published in the United States by Ballantine Books, a division of Random House, Inc., New York, and distributed in Canada by Random House of Canada Limited, Toronto.

Library of Congress Catalog Card Number: 68-18770

ISBN 0-345-39226-4

This edition published by arrangement with William Morrow and Company, Inc.

Manufactured in the United States of America

First Ballantine Books Edition: August 1995

10   9   8   7   6   5   4   3   2   1

Foreword

Not enough Texans appreciate the fact that one of their true pioneers lives in Corpus Christi. This is regretfully so because Dr. John Pilcher's pioneering is in the still badly neglected field of forensic medicine.

The mathematical probabilities are overwhelming that the death of every reader of this book will raise legal problems. His death may involve the payment of double indemnity accidental death benefits on an insurance policy. This same policy may contain a suicide exclusion clause which means that the company doesn't pay the beneficiaries one nickel if the deceased commits suicide within two years after the policy goes into effect.

There may also be a valid legal question of death payments under workmen compensation laws; or wrongful death lawsuits arising out of automobile or other accidents. Many deaths also bring up strange but vital inheritance problems; and we haven't even mentioned homicide!

The law has four categories into which all deaths fit: *natural causes, accident, homicide or suicide.* This classification, however, just doesn't happen automatically. Perhaps as many as 30 percent of all deaths are extremely difficult to classify correctly. Some deaths that look for all the world like suicides are proved to be accidental, after expert investigation. It may turn out that the driver of an automobile suffered a heart attack before the accident, so that the accident was actually caused by the heart attack, rather than the heart attack being caused by the accident.

There are difficult *medical* questions; and the *medical cause of death* should always be made by a skilled and experienced specialist in *forensic medicine.*

Still, in Dr. Pilcher's home state of Texas, only four cities provide a Medical-Examiner system where this vital *medical* question *must* be made by a forensic pathologist. In the other areas of Texas, a Justice of the Peace acts ex officio as coroner; and it is up to this *non*medical man to see that the *medical* question is settled properly. Texas, of course, is not alone in adhering to the ancient coroner system. Thirty-nine other states have not progressed to the Medical-Examiner system.

John Pilcher first recognized the need for forensic medicine during his six-year tenure (1931-37) as Professor of Pathology at the University of Texas Medical School—Galveston Branch. When he went into private practice in Corpus Christi in 1937, he volunteered his medical services to the administration of justice.

"For many years," John Pilcher reminisces, "I was the only pathologist in southeast Texas, south of Houston and east of San Antonio, and had to cover any request for Forensic Pathology within a radius of 75 miles. At that time, autopsies for gunshot wounds, stabbing and so on were not considered necessary. The old-time sheriff in this region, or possibly the Justice of the Peace, could take a gross, eyeball look and see that the victim had been shot or stabbed; and that settled that. The sheriff then decided who was guilty before the case got to court; and as often as not, that also settled that!"

John Pilcher's case files read like the great mystery stories of all time. During one two-year period, his life was threatened; and on the advice of the prosecutor and judge, he carried a .45 revolver for self-protection. His colleagues called him the "pistol-packing pathologist."

"We're still fighting for a state-wide Medical-Examiner system," John Pilcher says, "so that more sophisticated medical and police science technics can be applied to the investigation of *all* deaths. There still aren't enough Forensic Pathologists to go around. We drastically need medical research in every facet of death. Only then will we be able to prevent many of the miscarriages of justice that take place now in both civil and criminal cases, because the facts of death were not properly investigated and evaluated."

John Pilcher's devoted wife, Etta Mae, has worked grueling hours beside him in the laboratory. She is an expert photographer and has taken the official pictures of many of his heartrending cases.

The Pilchers have visited my ranch. Our friendship began years ago when John and I became members of the American Academy of Forensic Sciences. I have admired his calm, deep, professional approach to the problems of death, which are really the problems of the living; and I sincerely appreciate his loyal friendship.

It, therefore, gives me genuine pleasure to dedicate this book to a modern pioneer in a vitally important field.

JOHN PILCHER, M.D.
Forensic Pathologist,
Corpus Christi, Texas

Erle Stanley Gardner

Chapter 1

Selma Anson pushed back her plate and drank the last of the coffee. She picked up the check which had been placed on the metal tray at the edge of the table, added up the amount, put at the bottom of the check: Tip 20%, signed her name and the number of her apartment.

As she arose from her chair, a man who had been eating a leisurely breakfast at a corner table put down the folded newspaper which he had been reading in between sips of his coffee, got to his feet, straightened his shoulders, buttoned his coat, and paused at the cashier's desk.

The man evidently had the exact change because he didn't have to wait but started moving casually out of the dining room, across the luxurious lobby of the apartment hotel, only a few feet behind Selma Anson.

She shortened her step.

The man hesitated near the door.

Selma Anson said, "Suppose you and I have a little talk."

The man kept his eyes focused on the street, apparently immersed in thought.

"I'm talking to *you*," she said.

The man gave a surprised start, turned and looked at Selma Anson as one would regard a perfect stranger who had shown symptoms of mental aberration.

"Don't try to play it innocent," she said. "You've been following me for something over a week now, keeping me under surveillance. I want to know what it's all about."

"I've been following you!" the man exclaimed.

"*You* have been following *me*," Selma Anson repeated firmly.

The man, somewhere in his early thirties, was of medium height and average build. He wore a dark gray business suit and a quiet tie. Hurrying through a subway entrance, he would not have received a second glance.

"I think there's been some mistake, madam," he said, and started to move away.

Selma Anson was in her early fifties. She had kept her figure, her poise, her sense of humor, and her proud independence. Since the death of her husband a year ago, she had prided herself upon living her own life as an individual. She frequently said, "I like what I like and not what I'm supposed to like because of some mass rating. And I very much dislike the things I don't like."

Right at the moment it appeared that the man to whom she was talking was one of the things that she didn't like.

"I don't know what the idea is," she said, "but you've been dogging my steps for the last week that I know of. Everywhere I go I see you, and I have gone to some places where I would not ordinarily have gone for the sole purpose of seeing if you would show up.

"You were always there.

"Now, I'm going to tell you something. I don't like to create a public scene. I don't know just what my rights are, but the next time I see you I'm going to slap your face. And after that, I'm going to slap your face *every* time I see you. That, I think, will cause enough commotion so that we'll find out what this is all about."

The man's eyes snapped with indignation. "You slap my face," he said, "and I'll teach you something about the law of assault and battery. I'll ask for compensatory damages and exemplary damages, and if you don't think I can do it and put a nick in that bankroll of yours, you just talk it over with any good lawyer."

With that, the man lunged at the revolving door, went out to the street and disappeared.

Chapter 2

Della Street, Perry Mason's confidential secretary said, "You have half an hour before your next appointment. Could you possibly see a Mrs. Selma Anson?"

Perry Mason frowned, looked up from the Supreme Court case he was reading, said, "What does she want, Della?"

"Someone's been following her and she wants to know what will happen if she slaps the man's face."

"A nut?" Mason asked.

Della Street shook her head. "She isn't the type given to imagining things; she isn't neurotic. She's just a sweet individual, but I have an idea she has a mind of her own. My best guess is that she's going to slap and slap hard."

"How old?"

"Early fifties."

"Money?"

"She's wearing thirty-dollar shoes. She has an alligator handbag. Her clothes are quiet but expensive. She's well-groomed and . . ."

"Chunky?" Mason interrupted.

"A very nice figure. She's quietly well-kept. Well . . . you have the feeling she's been through a lot and learned a lot."

"I'll see her," Mason said, "and talk with her long enough to get her story. But you know how it is, Della: so many people get to feeling that someone's following them, they want to see a lawyer, and the first thing you know you're tied up with some neurotic individual who becomes an office pest."

Della Street said indignantly, "What do you think you

pay me *my* salary for? I can weed those people out as far as I can see them."

Mason grinned. "All right, let's talk with Mrs. Anson and see how close you hit the nail on the head this time, Della. I only have a few minutes because of this other appointment."

Della Street nodded, went to the outer office and returned with Selma Anson.

"Mr. Mason," she said.

Selma Anson briefly studied the lawyer's powerful frame, wavy hair, granite-hard features, then smiled.

"How do you do, Mr. Mason. I told your secretary generally what I wanted. Someone's been following me, and it's not that I'm imagining things. I understand you have an appointment within a few minutes.

"You're a busy man. You're going to want a retainer. I'm prepared to give you any reasonable retainer."

"And just what do you want?" Mason asked. "What do you expect me to do? But please sit down, Mrs. Anson."

She seated herself in the client's chair and said, "I put up with this man just as long as I could stand him.

"This morning I was having breakfast in the dining room of my apartment hotel. He was there, keeping an eye on me, planning to see where I went today."

"What did you do?"

"I walked up to him and told him that I was sick and tired of having him follow me around, that if I saw any more of him I was going to slap his face and keep on slapping it every time I saw him."

"And what did he say to that?" Mason asked.

"He said that I'd better see an attorney and find out what would happen to me. He said that he would sue me for actual damages and—some other kind of damages."

"Exemplary damages?" Mason asked.

"I guess so, yes. Could he collect double damages?"

"It depends on the facts," Mason said. "Compensatory damages are awarded to compensate a person for another's wrongful act. Exemplary damages or punitive damages, as

4

they are sometimes called, are imposed upon a person who has injured another under circumstances of deliberate wrongdoing or oppression. Such damages are awarded as a means of punishing the wrongdoer and setting an example to others who might be tempted to do the same thing."

"How much would they be?" she asked.

"How much would what be?"

"These punitive or exemplary damages you talk about."

Mason laughed and said, "You really mean that you're going to slap his face, Mrs. Anson?"

"I really mean it."

"I would advise you not to, at least until we know more about the situation. If he has actually been following you, a jury might very well feel you were entitled to slap his face, but . . ."

"It isn't something I've been imagining."

Mason glanced at his watch, said, "Paul Drake of the Drake Detective Agency has his office on the same floor here in this building. He does most of my detective work.

"I would suggest that you consult him and have him put an operative on the case to shadow the person who is shadowing you, find out about him, find out where he goes, find out, if possible, whether he's someone who is a little demented, whether he's just trying to strike up an acquaintanceship, or whether he's a private detective employed by someone, and if so, who employed him. Any reason anyone would want to put a detective on your trail?"

"Not that I know of."

"You're a widow? How do you live? Do you keep pretty much to yourself? Do you have a circle of friends? Do you . . . ?"

"I'm a widow," she said. "I've been a widow for a year. I'm trying to live my own life. I'm interested in the theater. I go to the shows. There are some television shows I like, and a lot I don't like. I like books, and I go to the library and spend an evening reading every once in a while."

"Do you drive your own car?"

"I don't own a car. I use taxicabs when I want to go any-

5

where around the city. And when I want to go out in the country, which I quite frequently do, I rent a car with a driver."

"Always from the same agency?"

"Yes."

"And do you think you've been followed when you've been out in some of these rented cars?"

"I'm sure of it."

"By the same man?"

"I think so, yes. Sometimes I don't get a good look at him. Sometimes I do."

"Did he follow you here?"

"I don't think so. I didn't see him. I think I frightened him this morning. Somehow I have the impression that he's a man who wouldn't like to be the center of a scene."

Mason grinned. "A man would have to be something of an exhibitionist to welcome having a woman walk up in public and slap his face."

"That's what I intend to do. You're busy. Your time's valuable. You think I should have a private detective. How much is the detective going to cost?"

"Probably around fifty dollars a day. Can you afford that?"

"Yes."

"Do you want me to get you in touch with Paul Drake?"

"Could he come in here?"

"If he's available," Mason said.

"I'd like to have it that way. I'd like to have you sit in on the arrangements. How much are you going to charge me?"

"You could give me a retainer of a hundred dollars," Mason said. "There won't be any further charge unless something unforeseen develops. But I'll advise you and keep in touch with Paul Drake."

"Fair enough," she said, and opened her purse.

Mason flashed a glance at Della Street and nodded.

Della Street went to the telephone, called the Drake Detective Agency, and after a moment, said, "Paul Drake is on his way here."

Mrs. Anson had taken out a checkbook and a fountain pen and was making out a check to Perry Mason.

She handed it to him and said, "Fifty dollars a day for the detective. How many days?"

"Probably not over two or three," Mason said. "You'd better discuss that with Paul Drake. He'll be here in just a moment. Here he is now."

Drake's code knock sounded on the door and Della Street let him in. Mrs. Anson kept writing in her checkbook.

"Mrs. Anson," Mason said by way of introduction, "this is Paul Drake of the Drake Detective Agency. He's competent. He's honest. And you can trust him just as you can trust a lawyer or a doctor."

"How do you do, Mr. Drake," she said.

Drake bowed an acknowledgment, mumbled, with the words all running together, "Pleasedtomeetyou, Mrs. Anson."

Mason said, "Paul, we're working against time. I have another appointment in a few minutes.

"Mrs. Anson has a problem. Someone has been following her for something over a week. He has probably been following her longer than that, but she's been aware of it for the last week.

"She confronted him this morning in the dining room of the apartment hotel where she lives, told him she was going to slap his face if he didn't quit following her and she was going to keep on slapping his face every time she saw him."

Drake grinned.

"He threatened to sue her," Mason went on, "and suggested she'd better see a lawyer, so she came here. I told her that I would advise her to get a detective and shadow the man who is doing the shadowing. Got a good operative you can put on the job, Paul?"

7

Drake nodded, said, "O.K. We shadow the shadow; then what?"

"If possible," Mason said, "we find out whether he's a pest, a nut, or a private detective. If he's a private detective, we try to find out to whom he's reporting."

"That last will take a little doing," Drake said.

"If he *isn't* a private detective," Mason said, "your operative could pose as Mrs. Anson's brother, or perhaps a friend of her dead husband. If he's alert, aggressive and belligerent, he might frighten this shadow out of his wits and so dispose of the matter more or less offhand."

Drake looked at Mrs. Anson. "Can you describe this shadow?" he asked.

"I know every feature of him," she said. "He's a nondescript man who . . ."

"How does he dress?" Drake interrupted.

"Quietly."

"How tall?"

"About five feet eight, or five feet eight and a half."

"How old?"

"Perhaps thirty to thirty-five."

"How much does he weigh?"

"Oh, say a hundred and fifty or a hundred and sixty."

"Did you notice his necktie?"

"Yes, he wears a subdued shade and his clothes are always very quiet, cut conservatively."

"Sounds like a professional detective to me," Drake said, "and yet there's something strange about it."

"Why?"

"He isn't dressed like a rough shadow."

"What's a rough shadow?" she asked.

Drake looked at Perry Mason, said, "You tell her, Perry."

Mason said, "There are two types of shadows in the detective business, Mrs. Anson. The smooth shadow is rather difficult to detect. He makes it a point to keep out of the way of the subject. If he thinks he has been observed, he telephones his office and they put another man on the job right away.

"The rough shadow, on the other hand, is one who *tries* to let the subject know that he's being shadowed. He does everything that the subject would expect a detective to do, and does it in such a manner that sooner or later the subject notices him."

"But why in the world would anyone want to use a rough shadow?" Mrs. Anson asked.

Mason smiled. "They work in pairs."

"What do you mean?"

"A rough shadow and a roper."

"What's a roper?"

"A roper," Mason said, "is someone who gets the confidence of the subject, a somewhat casual acquaintance who will let the contact develop into a quick friendship."

"I don't form quick friendships," Mrs. Anson said.

"Well, we'll look at it this way," Mason said. "Suppose you meet a person casually who has exactly the same interests that you have, who is quick, perceptive and sympathetic. It would hardly occur to you that someone has studied your character, your interests, your tastes and then planted a person who deliberately leads you to believe that he or she has exactly the same tastes, the same prejudices, the same likes, the same dislikes.

"Circumstances develop so you see quite a bit of this person for a few days. That person may well be a roper."

"Go ahead," Selma Anson said.

"Then," Mason said, "at the proper time, the roper signals the rough shadow. The rough shadow starts dogging the steps of the subject until the subject will turn to the roper and say, 'Do you see that man who's following us? He's been following me for two or three days now.'

"Or if the subject doesn't bring the matter to a head, the roper will say, 'Look at that person who's following us. Don't turn your head right now, but wait until we come to the corner, then take a good look at him. I think he's following us.'"

"And then what?" Selma Anson said, her manner showing her keen interest.

"Then," Mason said, "the matter will be permitted to drop for a little while, but perhaps the next day the rough shadow will be on the job again and the roper will say, 'There's that man again.' Then you'll start talking, and the subject will say, 'Goodness, I don't know why any person should be following *me*.' And the roper will look thoughtful for a moment and say, 'Well, there's just a chance that he's following *me*.'

" 'Good heavens, why?' the subject will ask.

"That's when the roper does his stuff. Let's suppose that the subject is suspected of poisoning cats."

"Cats!" Selma Anson exclaimed.

"Cats," Mason said. "Poisoning cats."

Mrs. Anson frowned.

"So," Mason said, "the roper will say, 'Perhaps he's following me. You know there are people in my neighborhood who rather suspect me of poisoning cats. Actually I hate cats and people know it, and someone in the neighborhood has been poisoning cats and I think some of the neighbors suspect me. I just wonder if that man is shadowing me, trying to get evidence. Last week there was a very valuable cat that was poisoned and the owner actually threatened me to my face, accusing me of having put out cat poison.' "

Selma Anson was all attention now.

"Then," Mason said, "the subject will be pretty apt to turn to the roper and say, 'Did you?'

"And the roper will say, 'All right, I'll tell you. I wouldn't tell anybody else, but, actually, I did. I hate cats. They're destructive. They hang around the place, and they kill the birds I am trying to tame. I have a window feeder and the darling little birds come there and ask for their meals just as regularly as clockwork. I put out feed for them and watch them and get a tremendous kick out of it.

" 'Then the cats found out about it and it seems that every cat in the neighborhood makes it a point to hang around my place. I think people should take care of their cats and shouldn't just let them wander around.

" 'When a person has a dog, he tries to know where the

dog is. He doesn't want him just wandering loose around the neighborhood. But with a cat, they simply wash their hands of all responsibility and let the horrid little animals lie in wait in my shrubbery and pounce on my tame birds. I told the neighbors that I was feeding birds and to keep their cats home, and when they didn't do it I got some poison and put it in meat and scattered it around the place and I hope every blessed cat that comes on my place, trying to kill birds, gets poisoned.' "

"And then?" Selma Anson asked, her face frozen with interest.

"Then," Mason said, "the subject will say, 'Well, good heavens, we seem to have *all* of our tastes in common. As a matter of fact, *I've* been feeding birds with a window feeder and taking their pictures with a strobe light through the window. I've got some beautiful bird pictures and the cats have moved in on me and—well, I haven't gone as far as you did, but I did put out some poison for one of the most offensive of all the cats, one that just made a habit of hanging around my place.'

"Then the roper will say, 'Do you have any trouble getting poison?' And the subject will go ahead and give all the details of where the poison was purchased, where it is kept, how much of a dosage is given, and all of that.

"The roper is, of course, a very clever private detective, who probably has a concealed recorder which takes down everything the subject says in confessing to the cat poisoning. Such a procedure is expensive, of course, but there are times when people are willing to put out the money that is required in order to get an ironclad case."

"I see," Selma Anson said, her voice without expression.

"Have you," Mason asked, "made a new friend lately, anyone in whom you've confided or might confide?"

Selma Anson was thoughtful. After a moment's silence she said, "Well, yes, in a way."

"Who?" Mason asked.

Mrs. Anson said, "I was going to attend a lecture on Mexico and the early Mayan civilization. I wanted to know something generally about it and went to the library and got out some books dealing with Yucatán.

"This woman who came in and sat at the other side of the table was also reading books on Yucatán. She noticed what I was reading. I noticed what she was reading. We smiled, and I told her I was cramming for the lecture I was attending that night, and it turned out that she was going to the same lecture and was doing the same thing."

"What was her name?" Mason asked.

"Dorothy Gregg."

"How old?"

"About my age."

"Married or single?"

"A widow."

"You've been seeing something of her?"

"We had some coffee and a waffle after the lecture, and I invited her to have cocktails with me tonight."

"Dinner?"

"I have a dinner date."

Mason raised his eyebrows.

Selma Anson suddenly changed the subject. "All right, Mr. Drake, everyone is busy here, and Mr. Mason is squeezing me in, in between appointments, which I certainly appreciate. How much money do I give you, and when do we start?"

"You'd better give me a hundred and fifty dollars," Drake said. "My man will cost you fifty dollars a day and expenses—taxicabs, and things of that sort.

"He'll pick you up when you leave the building here and keep you under surveillance. When this man shows up who has been shadowing you, take out your handkerchief and wipe your right eye as though you had something in it. Put your handkerchief away and look directly at the man for a moment; then look away."

"What do I do after that?"

"Nothing," Drake said.

Selma Anson got to her feet. "It's been perfectly wonderful of you gentlemen to see me on short notice this way, and I want you to know I appreciate it.

"Mr. Mason gave me the name of your business, the Drake Detective Agency, and I made a check for two hundred dollars when I was making out Mr. Mason's check for a retainer.

"Now, I suppose you'll want me to stop in at your office so your operative can see me and we can get acquainted . . ."

"On the contrary," Drake said, "I think it'll be better if you don't know who my operative is."

"But I'll know when he starts shadowing me."

"Not *my* operative," Drake said, "and he isn't going to be shadowing you, he's going to be shadowing your shadow."

"So what do I do?" she asked.

"Just a moment," Drake said.

He picked up Mason's telephone, hurriedly dialed a number, said, "Paul Drake speaking. Thirty-two, eighty-six, ninety-one, immediate," and hung up the telephone.

"My, you sound mysterious," Selma Anson said.

Drake laughed. "It's just an act we put on. Would you like to walk to the elevator with me, Mrs. Anson?"

She smiled, "So your man can pick me out?"

Drake shook his head.

"Come now," she said, "he'll ride down on the elevator with me and I'm not so naïve that I . . ."

"I'll ride down on the elevator with you," Drake said, "and buy a cigar at the cigarstand in the lobby."

"I see," she said.

Drake got to his feet and held the door open, "Shall we go?"

Chapter 3

It was two and a half days before Mason heard any more of the case of the mysterious shadow. Then Paul Drake sounded his code knock on the exit door from Mason's private office, and Della Street unlatched the springlock to let the detective in.

Paul Drake, tall, loose-jointed, inclined to mask a tender heart beneath a layer of cynical sophistication, settled himself in the overstuffed leather chair and said, "Well, I suppose you want to hear about that shadowing case?"

"What about it?" Mason asked.

"I think we've got it buttoned up."

"Do you want to report to your client and then have her report to me, Paul?"

"I've already reported to her, Perry. She wanted me to tell you what I'd found out. I have an idea your client is holding something back."

Mason said, "You can say that for about ninety percent of the clients who come to a lawyer's office, Paul. I wonder if patients hold out on their doctors. They come to a professional man to get help and then they almost invariably try to color the facts. What is it with Selma Anson? Was there really a shadow?"

"There was a shadow all right. She wasn't imagining things."

"What was it, Paul, a rough shadow, or some variation of the rough shadow game?"

Drake shook his head. "Guess again, Perry."

"He could hardly have been a professional, competent private detective," Mason said.

"He wasn't."

"What was he?"

"A damned amateur."

"Your man spotted him?"

"Not for a while," Drake said. "Your Mrs. Anson evidently threw a scare into the guy. She said she was going to slap his face the next time she saw him and she evidently meant it. The shadow kept his distance after that, but he was still trying to tail her when my man got on the job—but the guy had been frightened into the background and it took my man more than half a day to pick him up."

"Then what?"

"Then we started shadowing the shadow," Drake said. "There wasn't much difficulty once we got him spotted and pigeonholed. His name is Ralph Bell Baird, and, in place of renting a car for his shadowing, he used his own car.

"Well, of course, my man got the license number and telephoned in. We made a quick check on the license number, found out who the guy was and where he lives, which helped a lot.

"My man didn't need to shadow him all the time. He'd pick him up and keep him in sight while the guy was tailing your client; then when he'd start home my man had an ace in the hole in case Baird ever tried to cut corners— which he never did. Apparently it never occurred to Baird that others could play his own game.

"Taken by and large, it wasn't too hard to find out who Baird was working for, a fellow by the name of George Foster Findlay, 1035 Montrose Heights. That's an apartment house, the Montrose Arms. Baird goes there at the conclusion of each day's activity and reports to Findlay."

"And who's Findlay?" Mason asked.

"Now, there you've asked a question," Drake said. "I got the dope and reported to Mrs. Anson. The minute I told her that Baird was reporting to George Findlay she dried up on me.

"So, I told her all I'd found out about Ralph Baird. He's a real estate salesman, working on a commission basis, has an opportunity to work at the hours he chooses and can lay off when he wants to. He evidently took it on himself to shadow Mrs. Anson and make a report.

"Now, Findlay is twenty-eight years old. He's a car salesman at the U-Pick-Em used-car lot. The guy's unmarried, plays the field, spends money mighty fast—probably just as fast as he can make it, perhaps a little faster.

"I haven't had time to find out the connection between Baird and Findlay. Findlay could have sold Baird a car, or Baird might have sold Findlay some real estate.

"The point is there's some bond of friendship there. And it's probably founded on some sort of a business transaction.

"Anyhow, when I reported to Selma Anson that Ralph Baird was acting for George Findlay and passing information on to him, she stiffened up like a poker. Your client, Perry, is frightened.

"I told her that if she wanted us to find out more about George Findlay we could do it, but that it would cost her money, and, unless there was some particular reason, I didn't see why she should pay out that money.

"She thanked me and asked me for my final bill in the case, and told me that was all she wanted.

"I told her that if she wanted my man to discourage this shadow of hers, he could do it."

"How?" Mason asked.

Drake grinned. "There are lots of ways of doing that. One of the best ones is to have your operative get right on the tail of the subject and follow him around for an hour or so; then suddenly double back, grab the shadow and accuse him of shadowing the operative.

"You have an operative who's a big, strong guy who knows his way around and has been in a few rough and tumble barroom brawls, and by the time he takes a handful of the other guy's shirt, shakes him around a little bit, and perhaps goes so far as to rough him up, the guy is quite content to let well enough alone and start minding his own business from that point on."

"What did Mrs. Anson say?"

"She didn't want any of it. She told me that now that she knew what the score was, she could handle things."

"In other words, she knows George Findlay?"

"She didn't *say* so, but I *think* she does."

"Well," Mason said dubiously, "I don't like to charge her for services that aren't going to be of benefit to her—we can probably give her a rebate—you have her address, Della?"

Della Street nodded.

"Give her a ring," Mason said, "and tell her that Paul Drake has reported and that, under the circumstances, we can rebate everything except thirty-five dollars which will compensate us for the time we put in, in getting her in touch with Paul Drake."

Mason turned to Drake and said, "If she gets some money back from what she paid me, she may feel like having you go ahead and make a report on Findlay."

Drake shook his head. "My opinion is that she knows Findlay, and I just have a hunch, Perry, she knows what it's all about now."

"You mean the shadowing?"

"That's right, and she's frightened."

Mason said, "She's a quiet, refined, well-dressed, well-groomed widow. What would Findlay, or anyone else, expect to gain by putting a tail on her?"

"That's the puzzle," Drake admitted. "There's certainly nothing incriminating in the way she spends her time. She goes about minding her own business, but she *could* be meeting with someone in whom Findlay is interested."

"She didn't give you any clue?"

"She closed up like a clam," Drake said. "She wanted a bill closing out the account with the expenses, and I gave it to her and that was that."

"All right," Mason said, "we'll give her a ring and make her a rebate. Maybe she'll talk to me in greater detail."

"I doubt it," Drake said. "She's become very close-mouthed."

The detective stretched, yawned, heaved himself up out

17

of the chair, said, "Well, back to the old grind, Perry. Don't be in too much of a hurry to make a rebate until you find out what it's all about. My best guess is that you're going to see more of her."

Della Street flashed a smile at the detective, "Good work, Paul," she said.

"Thanks, beautiful!" Drake said, and walked out.

Mason nodded to Della Street and Della Street turned to the telephone.

The interoffice phone rang just as Della Street was about to place the call.

She lifted the receiver, said, "What is it, Gertie?" then raised her eyebrows in an exaggerated gesture of surprise so that Mason could be warned in advance.

She cupped her palm over the mouthpiece, turned to Perry Mason. "Guess who?" she asked.

"Surely not Selma Anson?"

"Yes."

"Ask Gertie if she seems upset. Paul Drake said she was frightened. I can't imagine her being frightened. I think Paul's mistaken."

Della Street removed her palm from the mouthpiece.

"How does she seem, Gertie? Is she—I see—She always says it is very urgent. . . . Impress upon her that it's difficult to see Mr. Mason without an appointment . . . I see . . . a real emergency, eh? . . . All right, I'll see what we can do, Gertie."

Della Street said to Mason, "She's upset. It's another emergency."

"So I gathered from your conversation with Gertie," Mason said. "What's the schedule, Della? It's time for the Smythe appointment, isn't it?"

"He's five minutes late right now."

"All right," Mason said, "bring her in. We'll keep Smythe waiting for five minutes if we have to—and let's hope what she wants really *is* urgent, because we're going to have to break this woman of the habit of coming in without an appointment."

Della Street hurried to the outer office and returned with Selma Anson.

Mason said, "My time is all filled up, Mrs. Anson. I have an appointment with a client who is a few minutes late at the moment and I can listen to you very briefly, but it will have to be short. Now, can you talk directly to the point?"

She nodded, seated herself in the client's chair, took a deep breath, looked Mason squarely in the eyes and said, "Paul Drake has found out the name of the man who is shadowing me."

"Skip that," Mason said. "Drake has already reported to me. I know generally what he found out."

"All right," she said. "Ralph Baird, the shadow, is a friend of George Findlay, a used-car salesman."

"And the name Findlay evidently means something to you?" Mason asked. "Drake told me that you stiffened up as soon as he reported there was a Findlay involved in the case."

"Listen, Mr. Mason," she said. "I know how busy you are. I know what an imposition it is for me to come in without an appointment and steal time from some other client. I will give it to you just as fast as I possibly can."

She was interrupted by the ringing of the telephone. Della Street answered it, said to Mason, "Mr. Smythe is in the office now."

Mason said, "Ask Gertie to explain to him that there's an emergency matter; that he was a little late and I'm going to have to ask him to wait for a couple of minutes."

Della Street relayed the message. Mason turned to Selma Anson.

"Oh," she said. "It's the craziest, the worst mixed up thing I ever got into. I'm a widow and I think I'm in love. His name is Delane Arlington. He's a wonderful man, a widower. He has no children. The only relatives are nephews and nieces, the children of two brothers, Douglas Arlington and Oliver Arlington.

"Douglas is dead?" Mason asked.

She nodded. "Both brothers and their wives are dead. But there are these nephews and nieces. Some are nice people. Some are not. Delane has been a widower for some seven years.

"Now, I enter the picture and, for the first time in years, Delane has become romantically inclined. One of the nieces thinks it's a wonderful thing. She's just as sweet and nice as she can be, but the other niece seems to feel that I am a predatory animal of some sort, that her uncle needs protection.

"I presume this niece, Mildred, could be a wonderful friend to those whom she liked, but she doesn't have a friendly attitude toward me. She wants to protect her uncle. She has an overly protective attitude toward him—and so I come right into her line of fire."

"And?" Mason prompted.

"And," Mrs. Anson said, "she's the girl friend of George Findlay. George Findlay, I think, feels that he has clear sailing, and he's getting ready to marry her. From all I can hear of George Findlay, he's the sort who would be a fortune hunter."

"And so?" Mason asked.

"And so," she said, "this man, Findlay, would like to strengthen his position with Mildred by finding out something about me that he could give Mildred to help poison her uncle's mind against me. He would dearly love to find out something that would convince the uncle I was a fortune hunter."

"Are you?" Mason asked.

"No."

"Are you rich?" Mason asked.

"I'm comfortably well fixed."

"What about Delane?"

"He's very wealthy."

"He might reach some understanding with the nieces and nephews on a financial basis."

"They want it all."

"You said one was nice about it?"

20

"That's Daphne. She says Delane made his money, that it's his money and he should be able to spend it the way he wants to. That if he wants to get married, it's certainly his privilege and she thinks it would be a fine thing for him."

"You've met her?"

"Daphne came and looked me up. She looked me right square in the eyes and told me what she was there for. That she wanted to find out whether I was a woman who would make her uncle happy, or whether I was a gold digger."

"Rather abrupt, wasn't it?" Mason asked.

"Not if you know Daphne. She's just a straight-from-the-shoulder, honest, sincere young woman."

"And the other one?"

"The other one is Mildred, the daughter of the other brother. She's just the opposite. She's undisciplined, selfish, shrewd, scheming and utterly ruthless. Now, I mustn't take up any more of your time, Mr. Mason, but I just wanted to tell you that, under the circumstances, I'm putting everything in your hands."

"What do you mean by everything?"

"My interests."

"Just what *are* your interests?" Mason asked, his eyes narrowing slightly.

"My happiness," she said.

"It would seem," Mason told her, "that that is between you and Delane Arlington. You don't come to a lawyer with things of that sort."

"I haven't time to explain," she said. "You haven't time to listen, but there are matters that . . . matters that . . ."

"Come on," Mason said, "out with it."

She took a deep breath. "George Findlay," she said, "told Mildred that I was just a gold digger."

"Go on," Mason said. "You've covered that before."

"And," she blurted, "that I had murdered my husband in order to get his insurance."

"Oh, oh!" Mason said.

She sat looking at him in taut-faced silence.

"Did you," Mason asked, "murder your husband?"

21

"Of course not."

"What was the cause of death?"

"The death certificate showed acute gastro-enteric disturbance due to food poisoning with complicating factors."

Mason frowned.

"That's just it," she said. "George Findlay took it on himself to go and look up the death certificate. He's been just simply horrid."

"How well do you know him?" Mason asked.

"I've met him," she said. "I know him when I see him. I've talked with him. But I haven't spent over twenty minutes with the man in my whole life. His style of attack is to keep in the background and snipe, snipe, snipe, making trouble at every opportunity.

"Now, then, I can't go on without telling you more details than you have time to listen to. I want you to protect my interests. The sky is the limit. I want you to hire Mr. Drake to do any investigative work that you think may be necessary. But I want to have one person and only one person at the helm. I didn't dare tell Mr. Drake any of this.

"I've made out a check for a thousand dollars, Mr. Mason. Here it is. I'm not going to keep you any longer. And I promise you that the next time I'll phone for an appointment. But I was too upset today to ... I just had to see you."

"Now, just a minute," Mason said. "Mr. Smythe was a few minutes late and it isn't going to hurt him to wait a little longer."

She shook her head resolutely, said, "There are too many details you'd have to know about, Mr. Mason. And I just wanted you to be on the job. Go ahead and represent me to the best of your ability."

Mason said, "I'm going to want addresses. I'm going to want the address of Delane Arlington and ..."

"Heavens, you're not going to call on *him*, are you?"

"Certainly not," Mason said. "But I want to know the various people who are involved. I want to know the addresses of the nephews and nieces. My receptionist out there, Gertie, will take down the names and addresses. Talk to her on your way out. You can go out through the entrance office."

Mason turned to Della Street. "All right, Della," he said. "Tell Mr. Smythe we'll see him now."

Chapter 4

Della Street said, "D. A. Arlington is in the office. There's a young woman with him. He didn't give her name. He simply said he wanted to see you upon a matter of great importance."

"Arlington—Arlington," Mason said. "The name rings a bell."

"Selma Anson's very mature boyfriend," Della Street said, "was named Delane Arlington. Do you suppose this is the same?"

"Good Lord!" Mason said. "Of course, it's the same. We'll be roped into running a matrimonial agency if we aren't careful. Now that certainly complicates the situation."

"What do you suppose he wants?" Della Street asked. "He said his business was so personal he could discuss it only with you."

Mason said, "That's the problem, Della. What are the ethics of the situation? If I'm representing Selma Anson, I can't very well represent Arlington at the same time—not without confiding in Selma Anson and getting her position—and somehow I have an idea that Arlington isn't going to want that.

"On the other hand, I'm not in a position to tell him that Selma Anson is my client—that is, if he doesn't know already. I have an idea that Selma Anson wants our relationship kept entirely confidential."

"And in the background," Della Street said, "is the boyfriend of Mildred, who insists that Selma Anson murdered her husband in order to collect the insurance and inherit the money."

"Well, let's see Mr. Arlington and see if he's the same

one. Ask him for his complete name and address, Della. Let's find out if he's the one."

Della Street picked up the telephone, said to Gertie in the reception room, "Gertie, get Mr. Arlington's address. Tell him that Mr. Mason will try to see him for a few moments but that we are very, very busy this morning and . . . oh, you have it? . . . I see . . . Well, tell him to wait for just a few moments."

Della Street hung up the phone and nodded at Mason. "Selma Anson gave us Delane Arlington's address and Gertie got D. A. Arlington's address when he came in this morning. So we know who he is now. The address is the same."

"All right," Mason said, "go out and bring them in, Della."

Della Street went to the outer office, returned in a few moments with a man of about fifty-five—straight as a ramrod, clean-cut, flat-waisted, a little on the slender side, the dark hair sprinkled with gray.

The young woman with him was about twenty-five—a blonde with large, steady, blue eyes which somehow gave an impression of straightforward sincerity.

Arlington marched forward, extended his hand and said, "Thank you for seeing us, Mr. Mason. I'm D. A. Arlington; this is my niece, Daphne. I am very well able to pay for your time as far as the financial basis is concerned; but the matter must be completely confidential. I want . . ."

Mason interrupted by holding up his hand. "Wait a moment," he said. "There are a few preliminaries we have to discuss first."

Daphne Arlington stepped forward, gave Mason her hand and a smile. She said, "Uncle Dee is impulsive, Mr. Mason."

"When I have a job to do, I want to do it and get it over with," Arlington said. "What are the preliminaries?"

Mason said, "In the first place, a lawyer—once he becomes successful—has about five times as much business as he can possibly handle. Therefore, he quite naturally exercises the right of selection in regard to the cases he takes. He tries to determine in advance how much time and effort will be expended on a case, and decides whether he wants to take it.

"Also bear in mind that a busy lawyer has many ramifications. For instance, I represent a couple of insurance companies. Before I can take any case, I'd have to ascertain that . . ."

"Now that's exactly where we may get into trouble," Arlington said, "because I want to talk to you about an insurance company."

"What company?" Mason asked.

"The Double Indemnity Accident and Life."

Mason was thoughtful for a moment, then said, "A lawyer has to talk with prospective clients in order to find out what the problem is; but if it should turn out he is representing conflicting interests, sometimes a statement made by a prospective client can become embarrassing.

"Now, I'm going to suggest this, Mr. Arlington. Tell me generally—very generally—what is bothering you and don't give me any information that you wouldn't be willing to give me if I were representing the Double Indemnity Accident and Life."

"*Are* you representing them?" Arlington asked, his manner suddenly bristling with potential hostility.

Mason smiled and said, "I am not under any annual retainer from them, but I believe I have represented some of the officials in personal matters. And we have had one case where the company was interested. But just tell me generally what it is about, Mr. Arlington, and then we'll look up our files and see to just what extent we're obligated."

Arlington, slightly mollified, said, "Do you know a man by the name of Herman J. Bolton, a representative of the Double Indemnity Accident and Life?"

Mason frowned and said, "I don't think so, but we'll look it up after you tell me where Mr. Bolton enters into the picture. We keep a filing drawer with an alphabetical list of the people with whom we are affiliated in a business

26

way from time to time. Just generally—very, very generally, Mr. Arlington, what's it all about?"

Arlington said, "I want to get married; and this man, Bolton—damn him, I'll . . ."

"Now, take it easy, Uncle Dee," Daphne said. "Don't get all worked up about it. You remember what the doctor told you about your blood pressure."

Arlington took a deep breath, relaxed somewhat, said, "Mr. Mason, this is just one of those things."

"Go ahead," Mason said. "We hear all sorts of stories in this business."

"Bill Anson was a friend of mine. He was in the real estate business. He wanted to sell me a piece of real estate and I was somewhat interested. It looked like a pretty good deal.

"I've been sort of a lone wolf for quite a few years now. I guess I've depended too much on the love and affection of relatives."

"What relatives?" Mason asked.

"The children of my dead brothers, Douglas and Oliver Arlington, generally, and particularly on Daphne here."

"How many children?" Mason asked.

"Four," Arlington said. "There's Daphne, my niece; her cousin, Mildred, daughter of Oliver; then the two sons of Douglas: Fowler Arlington, who's married to a mighty nice woman who looks after me just as if I was her own father; and a younger son, Marvin, who is also married."

"Go ahead," Mason invited. "Tell me what it's all about."

"Well, Fowler Arlington and his wife, Lolita, were giving a family barbecue and making my favorite dish—crab salad—in honor of my birthday.

"Bill Anson had a matter come up in connection with this property that was of considerable importance and he wanted to see me. So Fowler said, 'Why don't you invite Bill and his wife over for your birthday dinner, and you can have a chance to talk after dinner?' "

"Bill Anson *and* his wife?" Mason asked.

27

"Of course," Arlington said irritably. "You don't invite a man over for dinner that way without inviting his wife."

"And you had known his wife as well as Bill?" Mason asked.

"I'd met her," Arlington said, "but Fowler knew both Bill and Selma—that's Bill's wife—better than I did. They'd had some business dealings together and they were all friendly."

"Go ahead," Mason said.

"Well, that was a mighty unfortunate dinner party," Arlington went on. "Crab salad was my favorite, and Lolita had made a huge quantity of it. Only trouble is, when I get worked up in a business deal, I get all tense. Have a little trouble with blood pressure, Mr. Mason, particularly when I get on edge that way.

"There was something about this deal that I didn't like. I'd been prepared to go for it, but this thing came up with the question of a zoning ordinance on part of the property and I just didn't like it. I told Bill how I felt about it. He was disappointed. He was just the opposite of what I am. When he got worked up over something, he ate a lot of food, claimed it calmed his nerves.

"Well, the crab had become tainted in some way. Everybody got sick. I got sick and everybody else did. It wasn't Lolita's fault. I think it was the fault of the man who sold her the crabs. He insists that Lolita or Mildred left the crab salad out of the refrigerator too long. Both Mildred and Lolita had been at the hairdresser's that afternoon. It was a warm day and I guess one or the other did forget to put the salad back in the refrigerator after it was made. I don't know, but anyway everybody got sick. And Bill got a terrific dose of it, which proved to be fatal because he had some other kind of complications—some kind of an ulcer or something. Fowler had a doctor, and so did Daphne. It was a bad case of food poisoning, and one of those things we like to forget about.

"Naturally both Lolita and Mildred felt mighty bad about it. Mildred has a friend who is a lawyer, and he told her never to admit that she'd left the salad out of the refrigerator that afternoon. At least, that's the way I put things together. They were afraid of a lawsuit.

"Well, I saw quite a bit of Selma Anson after that. I felt in a way responsible; but she told me nothing we could do would bring Bill back to life again and . . ."

"Just a minute," Mason said. "How did it happen that you began to see so much of Mrs. Anson?"

"Under the circumstances," Arlington said, "I felt sort of obligated to go ahead with that real estate deal Bill had been working on. There was quite a commission involved for him, and the deal was at a point where I could go ahead with it and the commission would come into his estate. I felt that Selma might need the money. Which shows all I knew about Selma."

"What do you mean by that?" Mason asked.

"The woman's a business genius," Arlington said. "There was a hundred-grand insurance on Bill's life. She took that and the money she got from settling up Bill's estate; she went into real estate for herself. She also entered the stock market and she's been coining money ever since."

"How long ago did this happen?" Mason asked. "This dinner at which Mr. Anson was poisoned?"

"About thirteen months ago."

"And what was the insurance company?"

"I've told you," Arlington said impatiently, "the Double Indemnity Accident and Life."

"No," Mason said, "you told me that you were having trouble with this insurance company, but you didn't tell me it was the insurance company that carried the policy on Mr. Anson's life."

"Well, it was a hundred grand. They paid off without any fuss, but they're looking into the case all over again."

"And what caused them to do that?" Mason asked.

"It's a long story," Arlington said. "I went in on one of the real estate deals with Selma Anson, got to see quite a bit of her, found out what a really sensible, lovable person she was and . . . Well, damn it, Mason, I want to get married!"

"To Selma Anson?"

"Yes."

"Is there any reason why you *can't* get married?" Mason asked.

"There certainly is."

"What is it?"

"Selma."

"What do you mean by that?"

"She won't marry me."

"You mean she doesn't care for you in that way?" Mason asked.

"She loves him," Daphne said.

Arlington whirled to face her, frowned, said irritably, "She won't admit it to me."

"Perhaps I can supply some of the facts here," Daphne said. "The family is opposed to the match—bitterly opposed, I may say."

"On what grounds?" Mason asked.

"Do you," Daphne asked, "want the real grounds or do you want to know what they say the grounds are?"

"Why not tell me both?" Mason asked.

"The real grounds," Daphne said angrily, "are that the family is afraid Uncle Dee is going to get married, that he and Selma Anson will have a happy, congenial life together; and that if Uncle Dee passes away first, Selma Anson will inherit all of his money."

"And the ostensible reason?" Mason asked.

Daphne hesitated.

"Go ahead," Mason said.

"Well," Daphne said, "they feel that it wouldn't look too good for Uncle Dee to marry the widow of a man who died because of food poisoning—under the circumstances."

Mason turned to Arlington. "You've had a chance to see quite a bit of Selma Anson since her husband's death, and you've fallen in love with her."

"Yes."

"How long?"

"How long what?"

"How long have you been in love with her?"

"You can't tell when you get these things," Arlington said irritably. "After you get older, love isn't like getting a broken leg or something. You can't say, 'I fell in love at two-thirty-five P.M. on the afternoon of Thursday, the twentieth!' "

"How long?" Mason asked again.

"I tell you I don't know."

"About how long?"

"Oh, all right," Arlington said. "I knew I was in love with her within a couple of months after Bill's death, but I guess I was also in love with her a while before I was ready to admit it."

"Before Bill Anson's death?" Mason asked.

"What are you driving at? You're . . ."

"I'm not driving at anything," Mason said. "I'm trying to get the circumstances."

"I'm not a philanderer," Arlington said. "Bill Anson was my friend. I certainly thought he had done a wonderful job in picking Selma for a wife, but I wasn't getting any ideas, and I wasn't making any passes—if that's what you have in mind."

"That wasn't what I had in mind," Mason said. "That, evidently, is what has been in the back of *your* mind."

"Well, damn it," Arlington said, "there have been so many insinuations about things—Mildred particularly. She says it would make a scandal if I married Selma. And then—well, then along comes this insurance man."

"What was his name again?"

"Herman Bolton."

"All right, what does he want?"

"Well, he started making an investigation, talking with everybody who had been at that birthday party. Apparently the insurance company isn't entirely satisfied, despite the fact they paid off the claim. There is some talk about reopening the case. Can they do that, Mr. Mason?"

"It depends on circumstances," Mason said. "They could, of course, claim that the insurance money had been paid out under circumstances which entitled them to recover it."

"What circumstances?" Arlington asked.

Mason said, "There I'm not in a position to advise you. They might have paid out the money by mistake, by fraud, or . . ."

"Could they get the money back?"

"There again," Mason said, "you get into the question of evidence. They might be able to show that under certain circumstances the money had been wrongfully paid to Selma Anson, and that she was a constructive trustee holding the money for the benefit of the insurance company."

"What sort of circumstances?" Arlington asked.

Mason hesitated.

"That Selma Anson deliberately poisoned her husband," Daphne said firmly.

"Now I'm asking Mr. Mason!" Arlington said impatiently.

"And Mr. Mason doesn't want to come right out and tell you," Daphne said.

"Frankly," Mason said, "I don't know the facts. What gave you the idea, Miss Arlington?"

Daphne said, "The type of questions Bolton is asking. Bolton's apparent theory is that Bill Anson didn't die of food poisoning—that he became ill from food poisoning, that he was sick and was recovering when he was given a dose of active poison which turned out to be fatal."

Arlington said, "Don't say things like that, Daphne. We don't know what Bolton has in mind."

"Perhaps you don't, but I do," Daphne said.

"You mean Bolton has told you things he didn't tell me?" Arlington asked.

"I think perhaps he has told me more than he realized, in between the lines of what he actually said," Daphne said steadily. "You have to face these issues the way they are, Uncle Dee."

"All this would get me out of the frying pan into the

fire," Arlington said. "Selma never would marry me if the insurance company started any kind of gossip of that sort."

"They're not starting gossip," Daphne said. "But Bolton came right out and asked me about my symptoms, about the symptoms of the others, about how much crab salad had been eaten, and whether I knew who had left it sitting on the kitchen table while Mildred and Lolita were at the beauty shop that afternoon.

"He asked me what I knew about those illnesses, and asked me if it wasn't a fact that we all of us had minor digestive upsets and recovered rather quickly, and whether Bill Anson wasn't on the road to recovery when he had a sudden relapse and died."

"Well," Arlington said, "the cat's out of the bag now, Mr. Mason. That's what I want. I want you to throw the scare of their lives into this insurance company and get them to back up and lay off. I have enough troubles as it is."

"You feel that this investigation by the insurance company will have a tendency to keep Mrs. Anson from ever consenting to a marriage?"

"Of course it will. And I'll tell you something else—that woman isn't the kind that pushes her way in where she isn't wanted. Just as long as the family has this feeling of hostility, she isn't going to marry me."

"Of course," Mason said, "you could handle that by having a showdown with the family. You could tell them exactly what you intend to do financially; and you could, of course, point out that you are perfectly free to make a will which completely disinherits your nephews and nieces if you so desire."

"I wouldn't do that," Arlington said. "I wouldn't go that far. They're my family. They're the only family I'll ever have. But if I want to get married again and make a will, leaving my wife any amount of money that I want, I certainly want to be free to do it. I don't want to have a bunch of nieces and nephews telling me what I can do and what I can't do."

"They don't *all* feel that way," Daphne pointed out.

"But some of them do?" the lawyer asked.

She hesitated, then met his eyes frankly.

"Yes," she said. "Some of them do."

Mason said, "Under the circumstances, Mr. Arlington, I don't think I'm in a position to accept a retainer from you."

"Why not?"

"You don't have any action against the insurance company," Mason said. "The person who would have the action against the insurance company for defamation of character would be Selma Anson. You might suggest to her that she consult me, and I could probably be free to represent her. But you don't have a cause of action; you can't prove any damages."

"Can't prove damages?" Arlington snapped. "If that insurance company gabble-gabble-gabbles around here and starts a lot of gossip and Selma won't marry me because of that, they'll ruin the last years of my life."

"I'm looking at it from a standpoint of legal causation," Mason said. "And I'm looking at it from a standpoint of client personalities. I would probably be able to represent Selma Anson in a matter of this sort where I wouldn't be in a position to represent you."

Daphne said, "Come on, Uncle Dee, that's plain enough. Get Selma to come to Mr. Mason."

"I can't approach Selma about this," Delane Arlington said. "She doesn't know what this damned insurance detective is trying to dream up."

"How do you know she doesn't?" Mason asked.

"Because I can tell by the way she acts. She's worried about the other things, and she's worried about the family and the family attitude; but that's all she's worried about."

"Uncle Dee," Daphne said firmly, "you're getting all excited about this, and the doctor said you should relax and be calm. Now, *I'm* going to take it upon myself to have a talk with Selma Anson. I'm going to find out just how much she knows of what's going on.

"Come on. We've taken up enough of Mr. Mason's time."

Daphne got firmly to her feet.

Delane Arlington arose more slowly. "How much do we owe you, Mr. Mason?"

"Nothing," Mason said. "You made a general statement of the case to me. Understand that you told me nothing which was in professional confidence. You outlined only the circumstances of the type of employment you wanted. I have explained to you that I am not in a position to accept a retainer from you. I have tried to outline my position as definitely as possible."

"Then you can't do me a bit of good," Arlington said. "Because Selma certainly wouldn't employ an attorney to put a stop to this."

"You don't know what she'd do!" Daphne said. "Wait until I have a talk with her as one woman to another. Come on, Uncle Dee."

Arlington hesitated in the doorway. "I can give you any amount you need as a retainer," he said. "Any amount within reason."

Mason smiled and shook his head. "At least, not at the moment, Mr. Arlington. I don't think you have any cause of action. Selma Anson is the one who has the cause of action."

"I tell you, she wouldn't do anything about it!" Arlington snapped.

Daphne flashed Mason a smile, took her uncle's arm and piloted him out of the exit door.

Mason turned to Della Street.

"Now this," the lawyer said, after the door had clicked shut, "is a beautiful situation! Selma Anson comes to me and tells me a part of the story."

"It may be the only part she knows," Della said.

"It *may* be," Mason agreed. "But she's being shadowed, and an attempt is going to be made by the insurance company to prove that she murdered her husband."

"Inspired perhaps by a little anonymous telephone call from one of the members of the Arlington family who doesn't want to see Delane Arlington get married," Della Street suggested.

"That, of course," Mason said, "we don't know; but it's a probability. However, we get a situation where the insurance company decides to reopen the case; where a rough shadow appears in the picture; where a contact who might well be a smooth professional roper appears on the job and . . ."

"It would appear that someone among the nieces and nephews is playing a very shrewd game."

"A game in which we are going to be dealt cards?" Della asked.

"I think," Mason said, "we will be dealt cards. I think we will be seeing more of Selma Anson in the very near future, and I hope the cards which are dealt us have an ace or two. See if you can get Paul Drake for me, Della."

Della's nimble fingers flew over the dial on Mason's unlisted telephone, which furnished a direct and very private line into Drake's office.

A moment later, Della Street nodded to Mason, said into the phone, "The Chief wants to talk with you, Paul."

Mason took the instrument from Della Street's hand, said, "Paul, this Selma Anson case is going into high gear."

"Why, I thought that was all finished," Drake said.

"Mrs. Anson left me in charge of her affairs and told me to use my judgment," Mason said. "I'm using it. Now I want two people on the job right quick."

"What sort of people? What sort of a job?" Drake asked.

"We'll start with George Findlay," Mason said. "I want a roper, and I want a rough shadow on Ralph Baird."

"Wait a minute!" Drake said. "I don't get this. Usually you have the roper on the person who is being treated with the rough shadow; then the subject confides to the roper that he's being shadowed; the roper asks him why in the world anyone would want to shadow him; and the subject is supposed to blurt out his story."

"That's right," Mason said. "That's the technique we're going to follow this time, but with individual variations."

"All right. You want the roper for George Findlay. That shouldn't be hard to arrange."

"Get a good roper," Mason said, "a fellow about Findlay's own age—not too much older—the fast-action playboy type—a real fast worker.

"George Findlay is that type. He's a used-car salesman, a fast talker, a fast worker; and your roper can fit right into the picture with him. Probably there won't be any necessity for a long buildup."

"But you want the rough shadow on Ralph Baird," Drake said. "I don't get it!"

"I want the rough shadow on Ralph Baird," Mason told him.

"Starting when?"

"As of now."

"Okay. How rough?"

"Plenty rough," Mason said, and hung up.

The lawyer turned to Della. "If they want to play games," he said, "we can play games. Now then, Della, get me Selma Anson on the line."

"Through the switchboard?" she asked.

"If you have the number handy, dial it yourself from here," Mason said. "We're working against time."

After a few moments, Della Street said into the telephone, "Mrs. Anson, this is Mr. Mason's office. Mr. Mason wants to talk with you on a matter of some importance. Please hold the phone."

Mason took the telephone, said, "Mrs. Anson, there's always a possibility that your line is being tapped, so let's please be careful as far as our conversation is concerned."

"My line tapped?" she exclaimed incredulously.

"There's always that possibility," Mason said. "Now, I want to impress some things upon you. This whole matter may be more important than we realize, and may be a little more efficiently organized than seems to be the case at the present. I can't afford to take any chances.

"Now, listen carefully. You made a new acquaintance—a woman who was interested in Yucatán. You follow me?"

"Yes, yes, go on!"

"Be very, very careful what you say to that woman. Don't have anything to do with her for the next few days if you can avoid it without seeming to be rude. If you *do* see her, or for any reason have to be with her, act as though you were thoroughly at ease; be relaxed, but don't give out any information."

"Can you explain?" she asked.

"I can," Mason said, "but I don't think this is the time. Now then, sit tight. Don't get worried or frightened no matter what happens. Just sit tight, keep your head, and keep cool."

"Why?" she asked. "What in the world is this all about?"

Mason said, "You collected some insurance after your husband's death?"

"Why, yes. He had a policy and I collected on it."

"And what did you do with the money?"

"I invested it."

"Wisely?"

"Luckily."

"You made some profits?"

"I made some very, very substantial profits."

"Now," Mason said, "there's just a chance that the insurance people may try to claim that the money was wrongfully paid in the first place, and that your custody of that money was as a trustee for the insurance company—which entitles it not only to a return of the money, but to any profits which you have made from the use of that money."

"Why ... why ... why, they can't get away with anything like that!"

"I didn't say they were going to get away with it," Mason said. "I am telling you what they may try."

"Why that would ... that would be terrible!"

"Therefore," Mason said, "I am asking you to be careful. I want you to get in touch with me at any time in case there are any developments; and I want you to be very, very careful with whom you talk. Now then, has a man by the name of Bolton been in touch with you?"

"No. Who is he?"

"His name is Herman J. Bolton," Mason said. "He's representing the insurance company. He'll probably come to call on you. In the event he does, he will in all human probability be carrying a dispatch case, which he will put down casually but in close proximity to where you are talking. Then he will ask you to answer certain questions.

"He will have a tape recorder concealed in that dispatch case—one of those hidden tape recorders which are actuated by a supersensitive microphone.

"Now then, I want you to tell Mr. Bolton that you understand there is litigation pending and that, as one of the parties to the lawsuit, it would be unethical for him to have an interview with you unless your attorney is present. And, then, look him right in the eye and ask him if there is a tape recorder concealed in that dispatch case he has put down.

"Try to get an answer from him—either yes or no. He'll be pretty much embarrassed.

"You can be righteously indignant, order him out, and tell him that you will give him no interview except in the presence of your attorney. Can you do all of this?"

"I can do it all. But—Mr. Mason, this is most alarming!"

"Why is it alarming?"

"Well, I guess what I meant is it's just a terrific shock to me. I had thought that all of these things were all part of the past—that once they paid the policy there was no chance of any trouble about it. Isn't there some sort of statute of limitations which prevents digging things like this up?"

"We are dealing with a peculiar situation," Mason said. "They may claim that there was deliberate fraud, and that they were prevented by your chicanery from discovering the fraud until a few days ago. They may claim that your husband committed suicide and they *may* claim that your husband was murdered."

"That would be George Findlay's work," she said. "He's already planted that seed."

"Exactly!" Mason told her. "Now, keep your own counsel and don't confide in anyone. A rumor is one thing, a lawsuit is another."

"Very well," she said. "I'll try, but this is a most disturbing matter . . . knowing that the insurance company wants to get its money back—that would ruin me."

Mason said, "There are some things that I haven't told you yet—things that may come to light within the next few hours. I'm representing your interests to my best ability. Sit tight and use your head!

"Bye now!"

"Good-bye," she said faintly.

Mason hung up the phone.

"Shocked?" Della asked.

Mason said after a moment, "Frightened."

Chapter 5

Perry Mason entered the office Monday morning to find Della Street in a state of excitement.

"Did you hear the eight o'clock news on the radio?" she asked.

Mason shook his head. "Should I have been listening?"

"You would have received quite an earful," Della Street said.

"Shoot!"

"The District Attorney's office, in a surprise move, secured an order for the exhumation of the body of William Harper Anson, who died some thirteen months ago presumably from food poisoning. The announcer said that a preliminary examination indicated the presence of arsenic."

"Oh-oh!" Mason said.

"And," Della Street said, "the radio announcement indicated there was still other evidence in the possession of the authorities, which neither the police nor the District Attorney would communicate to the media because they did not wish to impair the defendant's chances of having a fair trial."

"The defendant?" Mason asked. "Did they name the proposed defendant?"

"No."

"That," Mason said, "is vicious propaganda. That is like saying 'for ethical reasons, we cannot state that a warrant is being issued for the widow and, therefore, we will make no statement about a further startling development in the case.' "

"You think they are going to issue a warrant?" she asked.

"You don't have a defendant in a case," Mason said,

"Until a warrant has been issued and someone taken into custody."

The lawyer stood frowning as he digested the information he had received.

The telephone rang.

Della Street picked it up, said, "Yes, Gertie?" then stiffened and said, "Just a minute. Put her on the line; Mr. Mason will want to talk with her."

Della Street turned to the lawyer.

"Selma Anson is calling. An insurance man by the name of Bolton has called on her and is asking her to make a statement as to facts concerning the death of her husband. She says that, in accordance with your instruction to say nothing, she . . ."

"Let me talk with her," Mason said.

The lawyer took the phone. "Hello, Mrs. Anson."

Her voice, thin and somewhat frightened, came over the wire. "Yes, Mr. Mason?"

"Mr. Bolton is there?"

"Yes."

"Tell him that you will make statements only in the presence of your attorney," Mason said.

The lawyer waited for a moment and heard her say to someone in the background, "I will make statements only in the presence of my attorney."

Then Selma Anson said, "Mr. Bolton wants to know if he can talk with you on the telephone?"

"Put him on," Mason said.

The voice of the man who came on the telephone was persuasive, filled with a subtle note of authority.

"Mr. Mason," he said, "I am representing the Double Indemnity Accident and Life."

"And your name?" Mason asked.

"Herman J. Bolton."

"Go ahead," Mason said.

"We are making a further investigation of the death of a policy holder of ours—William Harper Anson."

"And what about it?"

"The initial cause of death—or perhaps I should say the cause of death which was listed in the initial physician's certificate—was gastro-enteric disturbance caused by food poisoning and complications which resulted therefrom."

"All right," Mason said, "what about it?"

"The insurance company received some information which was rather disturbing, and I understand that the body has now been exhumed and that a preliminary examination indicates the presence of arsenic poisoning. Under the circumstances, it is very essential that we discover more about the circumstances under which the food which was supposed to be the cause of the poisoning was ingested."

"I see," Mason said.

"I have interviewed several of the people who were at the dinner, and have some very interesting statements. I now want to get a statement from Selma Anson, the surviving widow. She refuses to give it to me."

"She refused?" Mason asked.

"Well, she refused to make any statement except in the presence of her attorney."

"She didn't say that she wouldn't give you a statement?"

"She said that she would make no statement except in the presence of her attorney."

"That's not refusing to give a statement," Mason said. "If you have any questions to ask, you can come to my office with Selma Anson and we'll take it from there."

"It would seem that if she is acting in good faith," Bolton said, "she would have no reluctance to make a statement to the insurance company."

"All right," Mason said, "since you're talking about good faith, let me ask you what the insurance company is going to do."

"What do you mean what it's going to do? I don't know that it's going to do anything. It's making an investigation."

"And the reason it is making an investigation is that, under some circumstances, the insurance company believes that it can recover the amount that was paid under the policy?"

43

"That is a matter for the legal department. I am only in the department of investigation."

"But that is a reasonable supposition?" Mason asked.

"Well, I wouldn't say that it was outside the possibilities."

"Under such circumstances," Mason said, "the minute the issue gets into the hands of the legal department you have absolutely no right to talk with a litigant on the other side except in the presence of her attorney. And I would suggest that you have an insurance attorney present at the time of any interview *we* may have."

"Oh, bosh! That's not necessary!" Bolton said irritably. "I've been in the investigative business for years and, when it comes to asking questions, I tell the attorneys what to do rather than have them tell me what to do."

"I made the suggestion in the interest of ethics," Mason said. "I shouldn't talk with you except in the presence of an attorney for the insurance company. And very definitely you shouldn't talk with Selma Anson except in the presence of her attorney."

"When can we see you?" Bolton asked.

"Who do you mean by we?"

"Mrs. Anson and myself."

"No attorney?"

"No attorney. I have told you I don't need any assistance from the legal department of the insurance company in these matters."

"Get a letter from the attorneys for the insurance company," Mason said, "explaining that they are perfectly willing to have you questioned by me without any representative of the legal department of the insurance company present."

"But *you* aren't going to question *me*," Bolton said. "I am going to question Selma Anson."

"That's what you think!" Mason said. "If you think you're going to question Selma Anson without being willing to answer questions which I may ask, you might just as well quit right now."

44

"Very well," Bolton said. "*I* have nothing to conceal."

"*We* have nothing to conceal," Mason said. "But as you point out, you're very expert and very adroit in this type of thing, and we certainly aren't going to be placed in the position of lambs being led to the slaughter."

"That's a good one!" Bolton said. "Perry Mason, the famous attorney—a lamb being led to the slaughter!"

"You get your letter from the legal department of the insurance company and then call me back," Mason said. "Now put Selma Anson on the phone."

When Selma Anson had returned to the phone, Mason said, "Get rid of him, Mrs. Anson. Don't say a word about anything pertinent to the case. Simply say that you can make no comments except in the presence of your attorney. Get him out of there, and then call me back as soon as he has left. Make sure he has left and is out of earshot when you place the call.

"Do you understand?"

"I understand," she said.

"Okay," Mason said. "Get rid of him and call back."

The lawyer hung up the telephone.

Mason, waiting for Selma Anson's call, paced the office—tossing out words now and then to Della Street.

"This is a trick, Della . . . If the police were conducting the investigation, the minute it ceased to be a general investigation and tended to concentrate upon a particular individual, they would have to warn that individual—in this case, Selma Anson—that she was under suspicion of murder; that anything she said would be used against her; that she was entitled to an attorney at all stages of the proceedings."

"And as it is?" Della Street asked.

"As it is," Mason said, "they thought they would send this insurance investigator around to claim that he was investigating the circumstances of her husband's death; probably make some statements to her which would cause her to lose her temper and perhaps her head as well, and she'd make a lot of statements as to facts that she might be sorry for later.

"So this man found out that I was representing her and he dashed to the nearest telephone to notify his superiors and get instructions."

The phone rang.

"That'll be Mrs. Anson," Della Street said.

Mason nodded, moved over to the phone.

Della Street answered and said, "Just a moment, Mrs. Anson," and handed the phone to Mason.

Mason said, "Now listen, Mrs. Anson, this is important. This man, Bolton, is going to be back probably within a few minutes armed with an authorization from his company and the legal department, or perhaps from one of the officials of the company, to go right ahead with the investigation. He's going to suggest that you come up here to my office immediately."

"But we can't do that," she said. "I've caused you enough trouble coming in on emergency matters without appointments and . . ."

"That's quite all right," Mason said. "This is once I want to get going in the case before the other side has a chance to build it up."

"Who's the other side?" she asked.

"The insurance company for one, and the police for another."

"The police?"

"The police," Mason said. "Don't be naïve. If the insurance company could get enough evidence for the authorities to arrest you for poisoning your husband, the insurance company would then start suit to have you declared a trustee of the money that was paid to you and all of the profits that you have made by investing that money since it was paid.

"In order to make it stick, they'd have to show bad faith on your part; they'd have to show that the money was received because of misrepresentations made by you and because of fraudulent practices perpetrated by you. They'd have to show that they didn't discover the fraud and that, with reasonable diligence, they couldn't have discovered it.

46

"Now then, someone is making all the trouble for you that possibly can be made. I think you know who it is. Let's play things carefully.

"There's every chance that your phone may be bugged. I don't know. I'm having to take a chance telling you this much.

"When Mr. Bolton comes back, you telephone me for an appointment. I'll tell you to come to the office right away. You get out of there, and watch out for that dispatch case in case he's . . ."

"He has one. He came in with a leather dispatch case and put it down right beside his chair."

"A tape recording machine," Mason said. "You say absolutely nothing to him except the two words 'No Comment' until you get to my office, and then let me do the talking. Do you have that straight?"

"Yes."

"Okay," Mason said, "I'll be looking for you. Come right up just as soon as I tell you to."

Chapter 6

Della Street said, "They're here."

"You mean Selma Anson and the insurance man?"

She nodded.

"Show them in," Mason said.

Della Street went to the door leading to the reception room, opened it and ushered Selma Anson and a rather eager-beaver type of individual into the office.

Selma Anson hung back, as though she had been a child caught doing something naughty and sent to the principal's office.

The man, on the other hand, moved aggressively forward.

"How do you do, Mr. Mason?" he snapped. "I'm Herman J. Bolton, adjuster for the Double Indemnity Accident and Life. I think you understand the situation that brings me here."

Mason shook hands perfunctorily. "I've never gone in much for mental telepathy," he said, "so let's spell it out."

"My company had a hundred-thousand-dollar insurance policy on the life of William Harper Anson. The man died some thirteen months ago. There was no reason at the time to suggest anything other than a natural death in accordance with the provisions of the death certificate. We paid the claim. Mrs. Anson accepted the money and has, I believe, invested it very wisely. She has invested and re-invested and made very large profits."

"So?" Mason asked.

"Now," Bolton said, "we have reason to believe that our payment of the policy was premature, to say the least."

"What do you mean by premature?"

"We should have continued our investigations."

"And what do you expect a continuation of those investigations would have shown?"

"The possibility that we should not have paid the money to Mrs. Anson."

"On what ground?"

"I'll go into that in a moment."

"Very interesting," Mason said. "Do you have a letter from your company's lawyers saying it is all right for you to meet with me in their absence?"

"Not a letter, but I have their instructions over the phone. They said for you to call them if you weren't satisfied."

Selma Anson had eased herself into a chair. Bolton stood, his shoulders squared, throwing his words at Mason.

"You'd better sit down," Mason said, and seated himself comfortably in the swivel chair behind the desk.

Bolton hesitated for a moment, then seated himself on the edge of a chair on the other side of Mason's desk.

"Now then," Mason said, "you say that you may have made a mistake in a premature payment of the policy. What possible events could have changed the situation so that you would have been relieved from payment?"

"Suicide, for one thing," Bolton snapped.

"Didn't the policy provide that, after one year, payment would be made even if the person covered committed suicide?"

"On the contrary," Bolton stated, "this was one of those policies which provided that, in the event of suicide, there was no liability on the part of the company."

"What makes you think there was suicide?"

"I haven't said that I thought there was suicide. I said that a further investigation *might* have shown that there was a suicide."

"Committed in what manner?"

"I'll be frank with you," Bolton said. "You apparently want to deal at arm's length with us. We're working on a basis of friendship. We believe in perfect cooperation. I'm

49

not going to try to withhold information from you. How much do you know about arsenic poisoning?"

"Is that essential to what you are going to tell me?" Mason asked.

"It might save time if I knew."

"Let's not try to save time," Mason said. "We've got all the time in the world."

"Very well," Bolton said. "Arsenic is a very persistent type of poison. We know Anson died of arsenic poisoning and not from food poisoning."

"Go on," Mason said.

Bolton said, "It is, of course, possible that Anson—knowing that the provisions of his policy excluded death by suicide, wanting to take his own life and leave his widow well provided for—arranged to put arsenic in the food at a time when he attended a dinner with friends, using just enough arsenic in the dishes of the others so that they would have slight symptoms, putting enough in his own dish so that the result would be fatal.

"Under those circumstances, any attending physician would be inclined to diagnose Anson's sickness as that of food poisoning—a gastro-enteric disturbance which, coupled with problems of an ulcer, would result in a fatality with only a small amount of food poisoning."

"And, under those circumstances," Mason said, "it is your contention that the insurance company would not be liable."

"Exactly."

"And do you further contend that you could then try to repossess the money from the widow?"

"Now, that is up to the legal department," Bolton said, "and I'm not going to argue the legal possibilities with you. But, under certain circumstances, the principal of the policy *could* be repossessed."

"And under other circumstances it could not?"

"Under other circumstances," Bolton said, selecting his words carefully, "not only could the principal of the policy be repossessed, but it is the contention of our legal department that all of the profits derived from the investment of that principal would be the property of the insurance company and could be recovered by it."

"What circumstances?" Mason asked.

Bolton leaned forward in his chair, looked Mason squarely in the eyes and snapped the one word, "Murder!"

"Murder by whom?" Mason asked.

"By the beneficiary, Selma Anson."

"You are now accusing my client of murder?" Mason asked.

"No, no, no, not at all! Now don't get me wrong and don't try to put words in my mouth, Mr. Mason. I am simply discussing the legal points."

"Very well," Mason said. "Let's have it understood that we are discussing the legal points and that our discussion is impersonal. Could you explain your position in greater detail?"

"I see no reason to," Bolton said. "If a deceased is murdered by the beneficiary of an insurance policy, it is very well established that the murderer cannot take any property by reason of a wrongful act."

"But even that wouldn't make the policy void," Mason said.

"Now you're getting to a tricky legal point," Bolton said. "The policy is not void. The insurance company is called upon to pay the policy under its contract, but payment is paid to the estate of the decedent if there are heirs, and if there are no heirs, then to the state. I might refer you to the case of Meyer versus Johnson, 115 C.A. 646, 2 Pacific 2nd 456, and the case of West Coast Life Insurance versus Crawford, 58 C.A. 2nd 771, 138 P. 2nd 384."

"Evidently," Mason said smiling, "you have been briefed rather thoroughly on this by your legal department."

Bolton said, "I told you, Mr. Mason, that I have been in this business for many years and I think I am familiar with the fundamental principles of insurance law."

"Then just how does your company expect to reap any advantage by this investigation?" Mason asked.

"Simply this, and I admit it's a technical legal point. The Double Indemnity Accident and Life Company writes a very special type of policy. We are far more liberal in connection with double indemnities due to death by accidental causes than are other companies.

"In this case, for instance, the face of the policy was fifty thousand dollars. There could have been a question as to whether death was by accidental means in view of the fact that tainted food was voluntarily ingested by the decedent. However, the company raised no question on that point, because of our liberal insurance policy provisions, and we cheerfully paid the double indemnity. Mrs. Anson received a hundred thousand dollars, twice the face of the policy."

"Go on," Mason said. "Keep talking. You're doing fine."

"Now then," Bolton went on, "our investigations disclosed that, at the time of her husband's death, Mrs. Anson had no personal assets worthy of note, that she took the hundred thousand dollars received under the policy and started investing it. She has an uncanny aptitude for investments and she started pyramiding her profits. She invested in real estate and invested in the stock market, and she has run that hundred thousand dollars up to something in the vicinity of five hundred thousand dollars at the present time.

"Now then, if she murdered her husband—and mind you, Mr. Mason, I'm simply talking abstract legal problems at the present time. I am making no direct accusation. I repeat that *if* she murdered her husband, she perpetrated a fraud upon the insurance company when she collected the hundred thousand dollars and, therefore, she became the involuntary trustee for the insurance company.

"Under the policy of law which prohibits a wrongdoer from making a profit from his wrongful transactions, all of the gains that she has made would go to the insurance company.

"My company would, therefore, be in a position to receive five hundred thousand dollars by way of an accounting of which it would be obligated to pay one hundred thousand dollars to the estate of William Anson. Or, if there were no heirs, to the state of California. The remaining four hundred thousand dollars would be retained by the insurance company."

"Very tricky legal reasoning," Mason said. "Evidently the result of a lot of thought and investigation on your part."

Bolton said, "That's what my company pays me for, Mr. Mason. I may say with pardonable pride that my record shows I have saved my company many hundreds of thousands of dollars. In my investigative work I am a sharp-shooter."

"I see," Mason said. "By the way, do you have a tape recorder in that dispatch case?"

Bolton stiffened in his chair.

"Do you?" Mason asked.

"As a matter of fact, I do have," Bolton said, after some hesitancy. "I make it a point to have my reports completely accurate, and in order to lay the foundation for such accuracy in reconstructing what has been said, I like to check back over the exact words."

"I see," Mason said. "So, you want this to be a recorded interview?"

"Yes."

"As I understand it," Mason said, "the Ansons were guests and Mrs. Anson had nothing to do whatever with the preparation of the food which was served."

"She hasn't told me that in her own words," Bolton said.

"And you would like to have her tell you that?"

"Yes."

"And then you would question her as to how long she was in the house before the food was served, where the food was left, and all of that?"

"I probably would."

"And you have investigated this case up to this point quite thoroughly?"

"I have talked with various witnesses. Yes."

"You have talked with the Arlington family?"

"With some of them. Yes."

"In some detail?"

"Yes."

"And you asked them about where the food had been placed before it was served?"

"I understand that Selma Anson, your client, volunteered to assist in serving the food."

"I see," Mason said. "Under those circumstances I think that I would like to be in a position of equality with you before I participated in an interview of this sort where my client was called upon to answer questions."

"What do you mean by that?"

"I think that I would first like to talk with the other witnesses myself."

"That would be awkward."

"Or," Mason said with a disarming smile, "since you have a tape recorder with you whenever you are taking a statement from a witness, you can play the tapes which you have and let me listen to what the witnesses said."

"What are you talking about?" Bolton said indignantly. "Those tape recordings are my private property. I don't let anyone listen to them."

"It might make a great deal of difference," Mason said, "in how your questions were worded; whether you used leading questions, whether you put ideas into the minds of the people whom you were questioning, or whether you made a scrupulous attempt to be fair."

"I run my business my own way. I don't tell you how to run your business. And you aren't going to tell me how to run my business."

"Under those circumstances," Mason said, "there will be no statement."

"Now, that's not very smart of you," Bolton said. "We're making a good-faith investigation of the claim. There's a possibility of suicide, and there's a possibility of murder. Your client should be anxious to help us get at the true facts."

Mason smiled. "Remember," he said, "I'm not telling

you how to run your business. And you're not telling me how to run my business. As far as I'm concerned, the interview is over."

Selma Anson started to say something. Mason held up his hand.

Bolton continued to sit on the edge of the chair, his color heightened, his eyes angry. Mason said, "I will repeat. That is the end of the interview. I think you understand that. But, in the event you don't, you have your tape recorder to refresh your recollection. We will wish you good morning, Mr. Bolton."

Bolton said, "You can't brush me off this way."

"Why can't I?" Mason asked.

"Because I'm either going to get a statement from your client, or have her refuse to answer my questions."

Mason said, "She isn't refusing to answer your questions. I am refusing to let the interview continue at this point, and at this time. I want an opportunity to evaluate the evidence which you have in your possession before I instruct my client to answer your questions. She'll answer when I tell her to and not before. Is that clear?"

"That's not fair."

"I didn't ask if it was fair. I asked if it was clear."

"All right. It's clear," Bolton said.

"Thank you," Mason said, smiling. "We don't need to detain you any further."

Bolton angrily got to his feet, picked up his briefcase, said, "You'll regret this as long as you live, Mason. I've got enough evidence so I'm just about ready to make a report to my company. That report is distinctly unfavorable to your client. Her failure to answer questions, her failure to explain the circumstances, is, in my opinion, a very significant thing."

"What circumstances?" Mason asked.

Bolton said angrily, "I suppose you didn't know that your client has been buying arsenic."

"Buying arsenic?" Mason asked. "Are you sure?"

"Of course, I'm sure," Bolton said. "For some time she

has masked her homicidal plans by pretending to be very much interested in the mounting of birds.

"One of the best ways of keeping bird skins in a state of preservation so that the feathers do not fall out is by the use of arsenic compounds.

"There is a preparation on the market known as Featherfirm, which is used for that purpose, and Selma Anson bought large quantities of Featherfirm prior to the death of her husband. It may interest you to know that after the death of her husband Mrs. Anson seems to have lost interest in the mounting of birds, and, I understand, from the place where she made her previous purchases, she has not bought any Featherfirm since William Anson's death.

"Perhaps you'd like to explain *that*, Mr. Mason."

Mason looked at Selma Anson. Her underlip was quivering.

Mason strode to the door of his office and said, "I'll explain that at the proper time and to the proper people, but I am not going to have you come to my office under the guise of getting information and bully one of my clients."

"You're not going to tell me how to conduct an investigation," Bolton said.

Mason stood with his shoulders squared, standing between Bolton and Selma Anson. "Out," he said.

"You're going to regret this. I . . ."

"Out!"

"Very well," Bolton said. "Your actions convince me that there was no suicide, that William Anson was murdered, and that you know it, and that you're trying to protect . . ."

"Out!" Mason shouted, and moved aggressively forward.

Bolton fell back a step, turned and left the office.

Mason closed the door.

Selma Anson, taking a handkerchief from her purse, gave way to tears.

Mason glanced significantly at Della Street, picked up the telephone, said to the outer office, "We don't want to be disturbed under any circumstances, Gertie. And we can't see anyone until I give you the all-clear signal."

The lawyer walked back to his swivel chair, seated himself and said sympathetically, "Take it easy, Mrs. Anson. That man was deliberately trying to hound you into making some incriminating statement."

She nodded and said, "He's ruined my whole life."

"All right," Mason said, his voice sympathetic but insistent, "we don't know how much time we have before the police move in. You'd better tell me about this Featherfirm."

She said, "I had no idea—that—that just knocked me for a loop, Mr. Mason."

"I saw it did," he said, "and Bolton was preparing to use that as a bombshell. Now, suppose you tell me all about it."

She said, "When Bill was alive he was very much interested in real estate and he was an intense personality. I was left alone a good deal of the time.

"We had a beautiful house with spacious grounds and there were lots of birds. I got binoculars and started bird watching, and then, just as a hobby, I took up mounting certain types of birds.

"When I'd see a strange bird, I'd collect it."

"How?" Mason asked.

"I couldn't use a gun within the city limits, but I worked out a bird trap which was quite effective. If I caught birds that I didn't want, I'd release them. But when I caught a bird that I wanted, I'd kill it and mount it and—the man was quite right, I bought Featherfirm.

"That compound was recommended to me by the store where I got my materials."

"You bought a good deal of it?" Mason asked.

"I bought some. Yes. Several times."

"And after your husband's death?"

"After my husband's death," she said, "I saw things in a new light. I trapped a couple of birds which I wanted to collect, and then, after I got them out of the trap and had them in my hands, I simply didn't have the heart to kill them.

"Before that time I had been rather callous about such

matters. I was so interested in getting the bird properly classified and ... Well, after all, it was just a bird and I didn't think so much of taking the bird's life then as I do now."

"So you quit it after your husband died?"

"I gave up the hobby. Tell me, Mr. Mason, when you talked about the rough shadow and the roper, did you have some inside information?"

"What do you mean?"

"You were talking about the roper trying to get someone to admit to poisoning cats."

Mason's eyes narrowed. "Do you, by any chance, poison cats?" he asked.

"Heavens no, Mr. Mason. But I did try to discourage cats from coming on the place. I fed the birds, and some of the neighborhood cats hung around. I used to shoo them away and I told the neighbors to please keep their cats at home.

"One of the neighbors had a cat which she was very fond of and the cat died. I know she thinks I poisoned it."

"You didn't?"

"Heavens no. I wouldn't poison a cat. In fact, right now, I wouldn't take life under any circumstances, but for a while I was so intent on my bird mounting that I didn't think anything of trapping and killing a few specimens. Not many, Mr. Mason, just a few of the specimens I wanted to keep."

"And where are those birds which you mounted?"

"They're in the house."

"Many of them?"

"I think about forty-five or fifty that I mounted and a lot more skins which are preserved but unmounted."

"Doesn't it take some skill to mount a bird?"

"It takes a lot of skill, Mr. Mason, but primarily a lot of patience. I had to learn by trial and error with a book of instructions and such tips as the store where I bought my supplies could give me. Some of my first work was rather crude if you look at it with the eye of an expert, but some of my later work was very good. I had a lot of patience, a

58

lot of time, and I—well, I love the work, and I loved to have the mounted birds in lifelike poses in my bedroom."

"I see," Mason said thoughtfully. "Now, I'm going to tell you something which may come as a shock to you, Mrs. Anson. You're going to be arrested and charged with the murder of your husband. You're going to have to sit tight and make absolutely no statement to anyone."

Selma Anson's jaw dropped. Her eyes showed she was losing her self-possession.

"Now don't get stampeded," Mason said. "I'm your lawyer. I'm handing it to you straight from the shoulder because events may start moving very rapidly.

"This man, Bolton, is a very shrewd operator. I think he's working hand-in-glove with the District Attorney's office. I think that *he's* making *this* investigation at the suggestion of the authorities because in that way he would have more latitude than the authorities would. The authorities would have to advise you of your rights and tell you that you are entitled to have an attorney present at all times. Whereas Bolton, as the investigator for the insurance company, could sneak in with his concealed tape recorder and get a statement from you which could be used against you."

Selma Anson was speechless for a few moments, then said simply the one word, "Murder?"

Mason nodded.

"I can't—I can't go through with anything like that, Mr. Mason. I . . . I'd die."

Mason said, "I'm telling you not to get stampeded. I'm telling you to keep your head. You've got to play it cool."

"But the idea that I would murder my husband . . . I couldn't kill anyone. I couldn't . . ."

"I'm not talking about whether you're guilty or not guilty," Mason said. "I'm talking about what's going to happen. In view of my conversation with Bolton, I think he's probably on the telephone right now reporting to the District Attorney's office that he's getting nowhere and telling them to go ahead.

"Now if anyone tries to interrogate you I want you to

59

state that you are represented by an attorney, that I am your attorney, that at all stages of any interrogation you want me to be present. I want you to state that I have instructed you to answer no questions unless I am present, hear the question, and specifically instruct you to answer it.

"Now, can you do that?"

"I can if I have to, yes. But—but, good heavens . . . Mr. Mason, I can't take in all this!"

"I know it," Mason said, "and you're going home now. Della Street is going to go with you. You're going to wait for the prosecution to make its next move."

"Can Miss Street stay with me?"

"Unfortunately, she can't," Mason said. "But she can take you home and see that you get there all right. You came in a taxi?"

"Yes."

Mason nodded to Della Street, "Go ahead, Della."

Della smiled at Mrs. Anson, "It's all right, Mrs. Anson," she said. "Just don't worry. Are you ready?"

As one in a dream Selma Anson got up and walked to the exit door. Della Street held it open for her.

Mrs. Anson started out into the corridor, turned abruptly, said, "Thank you, Mr. Mason. Thank you, thank you, thank you!"

Della Street took her arm. The door automatically clicked shut.

Mason waited until they were well down the corridor, then picked up the telephone and said to Gertie, "Get me Paul Drake right away."

Gertie put through the call.

Mason said, "Paul, this is Perry. Della Street just escorted Selma Anson to the elevator. Put a tail on her."

"Della?"

"Selma."

"I haven't got anyone I can use at the moment. It'll take me ten or fifteen minutes to . . ."

"That's all right," Mason said. "You have Selma Anson's address. Della Street is going to escort her to see that she

60

goes directly home. Put a man on the job and arrange a relief for him. I want her tailed around the clock."

"Think she's giving you a double cross?" Drake asked.

"I don't know," Mason said, "but I particularly want to know if any official-looking cars drive up and try to spirit her away. If it's an arrest and she gets panic-stricken and doesn't demand that her attorney be present, I want to be able to get on the phone, identify myself to the police, and insist that I be present."

"I get you," Drake said. "I'll arrange for the shadows. You think she may be arrested?"

"She *may* be arrested, but we'll talk that over later," Mason said, and hung up.

Chapter 7

Perry Mason was waiting for Della Street when she fitted her latchkey to the corridor door of his private office.

"How goes it, Della?" he asked.

She shook her head. "I hated to leave her. She should have someone with her."

"She shouldn't go to pieces to that extent," Mason said.

Della Street said, "I'm afraid there's more to this than we know about. She's terribly upset. Chief, do you suppose she actually did murder her husband?"

Mason said, "It's too early to tell, Della, but she's entitled to a defense no matter what she did. The law provides that an accused person has the right to counsel at all stages of the investigation and a trial by jury."

Della Street said, "But there's something that—perhaps the disclosure by the insurance man that she was using an arsenic compound—well, that knocked her for a loop."

"That's easily understood," Mason said. "Her husband was evidently a man who made big money and spent big money. When he died she was left without anything. This fifty-thousand-dollar double indemnity policy represented her only chance to salvage anything out of the mess. She took that money, invested it, and now apparently has a cool half million."

Della Street nodded. "Still I wouldn't like to be in her shoes. Tell me, Chief, did you arrange with Paul Drake to have somebody keep an eye on her place?"

Mason nodded. "We'll have somebody there every hour of the day and night for the next day or two."

"You don't think we should let her know that we have a guard there to protect her?"

Mason shook his head. "Not now. To tell you the truth, Della, I want to know exactly what she does. If she goes to see someone, I want to know who it is . . . And, in the meantime, Della, let's get some of this correspondence cleaned up."

Mason started dictating and continued until approximately three o'clock in the afternoon.

Mason's unlisted phone rang.

Della Street raised inquiring eyebrows at the lawyer.

Mason nodded.

Della Street picked up the instrument.

"Hello . . . yes, Paul . . . what time? . . . I see. I'd better put Perry on the line."

Mason took the phone. "What's new, Paul?"

Drake said, "Your party left her apartment hotel, took a taxicab, went to the Seventh Street branch of the Business and Professional Men's Bank, was in there for nearly half an hour, emerged and had the cab driver take her directly to 1035 Montrose Heights."

"Montrose Heights," Mason said. "That rings a bell. Isn't that . . ."

"That's where George Findlay lives," Drake said.

"You have a tail on Findlay?"

"Not yet. Remember, I'm putting a roper on him, and I have the operative, but we haven't been able as yet to make a convincing contact. I have a rough shadow on Ralph Baird."

"Selma Anson went by cab, Paul?"

"That's right."

"Did she discharge the cab?"

"No, she kept it waiting."

"Your man was where he could keep an eye on the situation?"

"Right. She went inside and was there for twenty-three minutes. Then she came out, got in the cab, and, at present, my man is following her out on La Brea, but he feels sure she's headed for the airport now."

"You can communicate with your man?" Mason asked.

"Yes, he has a phone in his car."

"Tell him under no circumstances to lose her," Mason said. "Tell him to just leave his car parked at the airport and take a chance on getting a citation for illegal parking or having his car towed away, but under no circumstances to lose sight of the subject."

"I'll tell him," Drake said.

"Keep me posted, Paul," Mason said, hung up the telephone and started drumming with the tips of his fingers on the edge of the desk.

"Bad?" Della Street asked.

"Bad," Mason said.

"How bad?" she asked.

Mason said, "She went to the bank, emerged from the bank, went to call on George Findlay, and is now, apparently, en route to the airport."

"Good heavens, Chief, you don't suppose she's trying to buy him off or—or resorting to flight?"

"If she's resorting to flight," Mason said, "we're licked. Flight is evidence of guilt. Bolton can show that he virtually accused her of murder and if she resorted to flight after that accusation was made . . . well, you can see what it would mean."

"But she couldn't," Della Street said. "She's a well-poised, hardheaded businesswoman."

"She was well poised until the evidence of that arsenic came up," Mason said, "and then she went all to pieces. How did she seem when you drove back with her, Della?"

"Almost on the verge of hysterics," Della Street said. "She was shaking like a leaf. When she went into her apartment her hand which held the key was shaking so she had to steady it with the other hand in order to get the key in the lock."

"You noticed that?"

"Of course I noticed that."

"Then forget it."

Della Street smiled. "I make my reports to you—exclusively."

Mason said, "Good girl," got to his feet and started pacing the floor.

Della Street followed him with worried eyes.

At length Mason said, "Well, I suppose while we're waiting we should be able to get a few pages of that brief done. Hang it, Della, I don't feel like dictating or concentrating. There's something in this case we don't know about and I have a feeling that we're riding full-speed into a roadblock."

"Well, we could at least try working on the brief," Della Street said. "It'll probably be another five or ten minutes before we hear anything more."

Mason sighed, walked back to his office chair, seated himself at his desk, said, "All right, Della, let's see, where were we?"

Della Street read the last paragraph Mason had dictated.

Mason made two abortive attempts to get interested in what he was dictating, then pushed his chair back from the desk.

"There's something here," he said, "that we're overlooking, something that . . ."

The unlisted phone rang. Mason lunged across the desk and grabbed the instrument. "What is it, Paul?" he asked.

Paul Drake's voice, crisply businesslike, came over the wire. "Lots of things. Your Selma Anson paid off the taxicab, ran into the air terminal, didn't stop for tickets or anything but headed directly for the loading gates.

"My man followed.

"She passed up all the gates where people were waiting, but came to a gate where a plane was loading. She looked over the crowd, picked out a plainly dressed young woman, went up to her and said, 'Would it be worth a hundred and fifty dollars to you to sell me your ticket? I'll give you what you paid for it and a hundred-and-fifty-dollar bonus.'

"The woman grabbed at the chance. Selma Anson took the ticket, tore off the baggage checks, handed them to the young woman, then ran and boarded the plane.

"My man tried to board the plane, but they wouldn't let him on without a ticket, said the plane was full. So he picked up the woman who had sold her ticket to Selma Anson.

"This woman is Helen Ebb, 34 North Hamster Drive. Her ticket was on a flight to El Paso, Texas, via Tucson, Arizona."

Mason said, "Paul, ring up your correspondent in El Paso, Texas. Give him a description of Selma Anson, the airline, the flight number, and . . .

"Were seats assigned on that flight?"

"That's right. Seats were assigned. Helen Ebb had Seat 7A."

"The plane stops in Tucson?"

"Yes."

"Have a man get aboard the plane at Tucson and keep her under surveillance," Mason said. "Use bribery or any subterfuge you have to. Get it?"

"Got it," Drake said.

Mason hung up the phone, turned to Della Street. "Run out to the other office, Della. You take one phone, have Gertie take the other. Cover the airplane companies. Find out the first plane to El Paso. Minutes are precious. I'll be in Paul Drake's office for about five minutes."

Della Street nodded, grabbed a notebook, ran to the outer office.

Mason, his long legs working rapidly, shot out of the exit door and down the corridor to Paul Drake's office which was close to the elevator.

Mason jerked open the door of the outer office, said to the receptionist, "Anybody in with Paul?"

She shook her head.

"Tell him I'm coming," Mason said, and unlatched the gate which led to a veritable rabbit warren of offices.

Down at the end of a corridor, Drake had a little cubby-hole of an office.

Mason jerked the door open.

There was room for Paul Drake, a desk, four telephones on the desk, a radio receiver, two chairs and a filing case.

Mason wasted no time on preliminaries. "Paul, have your

operative follow Selma Anson when she gets off the plane. She's probably going to keep using the name on her ticket—Helen Ebb."

"She may get off at Tucson," Drake said.

"The ticket was to El Paso?" Mason asked.

"Right."

"I'll buy El Paso. I have an idea she's headed for the farthest point she can reach. She may leave El Paso for Mexico City. Keep a tail on her.

"Della and I are going to El Paso. We'll telephone you as soon as we get there. And call off your roper on Findlay and the rough shadow on Baird. Through a twist of events we're apt to be on the defensive for a while. I don't like it but that's the way the cookie crumbled. We'll call you from El Paso. Sit on the end of this phone until you hear from us. Keep the wires hot.

"Got it?"

Drake reached for a telephone. "Got it," he said. "This'll be another night when I have a soggy hamburger sandwich for dinner with a midnight snack of sodium bicarbonate. Have a good time, Perry."

Mason waved a sympathetic hand, opened the door and hurried down the corridor.

Della Street came in from the outer office as soon as the lawyer had entered his private office.

"Our best bet," she said, "is to get to Phoenix. If we hurry and if we're lucky we can catch a plane from Las Vegas to El Paso which stops in Phoenix. I've got Gertie on the phone arranging for reservations."

"Get Pinky," Mason said.

"I've already got Pinky," Della Street said. "She's landing with a two-motored plane at the Burbank airport. She'll be there by the time we get there."

"What's holding us back?" Mason asked, reaching for his hat.

Della Street, smiling sweetly, a coat over her arm, said, "You are."

Mason hurled the door open. "Let's go!"

Chapter 8

"Pinky" Brier, who did all of Mason's charter flying north of the Mexican border, seemed at first glance to be a young, carefree woman happily married to an indulgent husband.

Only on closer inspection did her well-shaped hands show their power, her eyes, the glint of steel. Even so the most observant would never guess she had ferried planes across the Atlantic in wartime and taught military aviation students how to use evasive tactics, or that she spent most of her time in the air, while her husband, an expert mechanic who worshipped the ground she walked on, saw to it that any plane she flew was manicured to mechanical perfection.

Pinky, flying a twin-motored Martin, made a perfect landing at the field just as Mason parked the car.

She came taxiing up, saw Mason and Della Street, swung the plane toward them, shut off only the right-hand motor and opened the door of the plane.

Mason and Della Street climbed aboard. Pinky started the right-hand motor, reported to the tower and started taxiing down the field.

"Phoenix?" she asked.

"Phoenix," Mason said, "and we're cutting it awfully close. If we don't make a connection with the Las Vegas plane at Phoenix, you're going to have to fly us on to El Paso."

"No sweat," Pinky said. "Can do."

She gunned the motors, worked the wing flaps, made the routine check, received takeoff instructions and was in the air.

Della Street settled back and said, "Well, we made it."

"So far," Mason said.

Pinky coaxed the plane into speed, flying over the congested basin, blue with haze, toward the towering mountains rising on the left. The late rays of the afternoon sun were casting long shadows on the ground beneath.

"You just happened to catch me," Pinky said. "I was just in from Las Vegas. I filled the tanks and took off."

Mason opened the bulky briefcase he was carrying, took out a very powerful pocket-size radio.

"Will it interfere with navigation if I get the news?" he asked.

Pinky shook her head. "We're in the clear now."

Mason said, "I want to get the six o'clock news broadcast if I can."

Pinky said, "Go right ahead. You've got thirty seconds. Remember that you lose an hour on this trip. Time's an hour later in El Paso than it is here."

"I know," Mason said, and tuned in the radio.

The voice of the announcer gave a summary of the international situation and comments on a head-on automobile collision which had taken the lives of five people, and then the announcer went on to say, "A Los Angeles heiress, who is wanted by the police for questioning in connection with the poison death of her husband some thirteen months ago, has mysteriously disappeared.

"Investigation shows that she went to her bank and drew a relatively large sum of money. She then went to the airport in a taxicab. At the airport, however, she seems to have vanished. There is no record of her having taken a plane out under her own name. Police feel that she used an assumed name.

"In this state, flight is evidence of guilt. The District Attorney's office wants her for questioning.

"Police refused to comment on the case against her. The District Attorney's office said, 'We want her for questioning.' Pressed further for details, the official smiled enigmatically and said simply, 'No comment.' "

Mason turned to Della Street, shut the radio off, and put it back in his briefcase.

"That was what you wanted?" Pinky asked.

"That was it," Mason said.

"And you're beating the police to it?"

Mason smiled, "I hope so."

Pinky flew through the pass with Mt. San Gorgonio towering on the left, San Jacinto on the right, both mountains having summits over two miles above sea level. Then they were over Palm Springs.

Mason pointed below to a line of palm trees which grew as straight as if they had been planted along a survey line.

Pinky nodded. "The San Andreas fault," she said.

"Cradle of the earthquakes?" Della Street asked.

"Cradle of the earthquakes," Mason said.

"Why the trees?"

"Water comes up from subterranean sources," Mason said. "I have an idea that if we knew more about that water, we'd know a lot more about the surface of the earth—and over there far to the right you can see the twilight on the Salton Sea, which is a body of water two hundred and thirty feet below sea level. There are strange things in the desert."

Della Street said, "I know how you love the desert, Chief, but can't you settle back and relax and get perhaps a few minutes' sleep?"

Mason shook his head, "I'm too keyed up, Della."

"Why do you suppose our client did such a fool thing?" she asked.

Mason said, "We know she went to see George Findlay before she left, and I have an idea George may be the villain in the piece. However, no matter what the reason is, we've simply *got* to get to her before the police do."

"What can we do when we get to her?"

Mason said, "I've got to think of something."

"You'll have to do *some* thinking," Della Street said.

"I know it," Mason admitted.

Della Street went on, "Going to the airport, buying the

70

ticket of a young woman, paying a hundred-and-fifty-dollar bonus. Chief, you don't think she's trying to run away and get to someplace like South America, do you?"

Mason shrugged his shoulders. "Clients do strange things," he said. "There are several things you can always depend on a client doing. A client will usually hold out some pertinent fact, will substitute his own judgment for yours, and then make some crazy move which affects his status without asking you about it in advance.

"Aside from that, you can't tell *what* a client will do. They're unpredictable."

Pinky grinned. "Remember I'm one of your clients, Perry."

"And," Mason told her, "you're unpredictable."

"I try to be," Pinky said demurely.

"Keep them guessing?" Della Street asked.

"Exactly," Pinky said. "It's one of our weapons."

They flew in silence while Mason, fascinated with the changing vista of the desert, watched the weird patterns of erosion in the buttes, the pastel colors, the long shadow patterns, the gathering darkness.

"I'd never make a flier," he said at length.

"Why?" Pinky asked.

"I'm too much interested in the scenery, particularly desert scenery."

"I know," Pinky said, "but lots of my passengers get bored with it. They think there's nothing down there except sand."

The dusk deepened as the plane crossed the Colorado River. Mason became less tense, propped his head against the headrest on the back of the seat, closed his eyes.

Pinky, listening in on the radio, said in a low voice to Della Street, "He's going to make it. The plane from Las Vegas is ten minutes late. We'll be there in time."

Mason straightened with a jerk. "We'll make it?" he asked.

"You'll make it," Pinky said.

Again Mason settled back.

Pinky flew steadily through the gathering darkness, then gently reached across to test Perry Mason's seat belt, nodded to Della Street, lowered the flaps and the plane descended at the Phoenix airport.

Mason, alerted by the descent, felt for his briefcase.

"You've got five minutes," Pinky said. "The plane's just coming in but it'll be five minutes at least before takeoff. I'm glad you've made it, but I'm sorry I'm not going to get to fly you to El Paso."

"We can save time on the jet liner," Mason said. "Otherwise, we'd have gone all the way with you."

The plane taxied up to the airport. Mason and Della Street climbed out of the plane. Della said, "I'll take care of the tickets, Perry," and raced to the desk.

Pinky saluted Mason with a wave of her hand from the cockpit, gunned the motors and taxied off down the runway.

The big plane from Las Vegas came gliding along, swept into a turn, followed the signals of a man with hand lights, and came to a stop.

Della Street came racing out. "Here we are," she said. "We have our tickets. The fact that we have no baggage facilitates matters greatly at this point."

They boarded the plane, settled themselves comfortably. Mason let the seat back and said, "Okay, Della, we've made it."

"Think we'll be in time?"

"I don't know," Mason said. "That radio broadcast will start things moving. This Helen Ebb, who sold her ticket to Selma Anson, will wake up to the fact that she figures in the act, and probably comment to a boyfriend somewhere. If he's heard the radio broadcast he'll get in touch with the police . . . Anyway, we've done not only the best we could, but just about all we could."

Mason closed his eyes, let his voice trail into silence as he said, "Now, we can relax."

The big plane glided into motion, paused at the end of the runway. The motors roared, tugging against the brakes, then abruptly the plane shot forward, left the ground and roared into speed.

Mason was still sleeping when they started their descent for El Paso.

Della Street nudged him, said, "We're coming in for a landing, Chief."

Mason opened his eyes, shook his head, said, "Uh," then smiled and said, "thanks, Della."

"Chief," she said, "if they can prove that Selma Anson bought that ticket and traveled under an assumed name, and if she was foolish enough to register under an assumed name in El Paso, what is there we can do about it?"

Mason said, "We'll have to use ingenuity, Della. After all, we don't *know* that she's here. She may have gone on to Mexico. She may have taken another plane east or north, or, as far as that's concerned, she could have doubled back to Las Vegas."

"Well," Della Street said, "you'll come up with something. You always do."

"Let's hope," Mason said. "A trial lawyer has to be prepared to cope with the unexpected."

The wheels touched the ground.

Mason said, "Get to a phone just as fast as you can, Della. Use your credit card and get a call through to Paul Drake. I'll talk with him when you get him on the line."

Della Street nodded, eased out into the aisle and, as soon as she was off the plane, hurried for the telephone booths.

Mason, carrying his briefcase, followed along behind, waited for less than a minute outside of the telephone booth. Della Street beckoned to him, opened the door and handed Mason the telephone. "Here's Paul," she said.

Mason said, "Hi, Paul. What's new?"

"You're in El Paso?"

"Yes."

"The subject is in El Paso. She evidently read the name that was on the ticket, Helen Ebb. She went to the Paso Del Norte Hotel and registered as Helen Ebb, of Los Angeles. She's in her room. I have a man on the job."

"That's fine," Mason said. "You can communicate with your man?"

"Yes, I can have him paged on the telephone."

"Page him," Mason said, "and take him off the job. Tell him to go home. What's the room number?"

"Fourteen twenty-seven."

"Had your hamburger?"

"Not yet. I can't seem to develop an appetite for a greasy hamburger."

"Go out and get yourself a good dinner," Mason said. "I'll take it from here."

Chapter 9

Mason held the door open for Della Street. They entered the lobby of the Paso Del Norte Hotel.

"We'll take a quick look around," Mason said.

They moved around the lobby, Mason making comments from time to time.

"This," he said, "is the great cattlemen's hotel. Enough cattle have been sold here to keep the world in meat for quite a while. Name any one of the famous cattlemen and they've stayed here at the hotel, put across deals and returned time after time.

"Some of the cattlemen were full of pranks. There was the well-known cattle baron who bought a wildcat in a cage over in Juarez, brought it across the line, and, when he was in a position to contemplate it soberly the next morning, realized that since he was checking out he had no more use for a wildcat than he did for a bicycle. So he got his baggage all out of the room, went back, opened the door of the cage, turned the wildcat loose, went out and closed the door.

"He never heard anything more about it until he returned a few months later to buy some more cattle. The clerk simply added a three-figure amount onto his bill as 'wildcat damage' and the cattleman never asked a question, never batted an eye, simply made out a voucher for the whole amount of the bill."

"Just what are we looking for?" Della Street asked.

"Inspiration," Mason said. "We've got to . . ." He stopped as a burst of applause sounded from someplace off the lobby.

Mason approached the clerk. "Any conventions?" he asked.

The clerk smiled and shook his head. "We're shy of conventions right at the moment."

"What's the applause?"

"Banquet."

"What banquet?"

"International Exchange Club. That's a club of prominent businessmen on this side of the line, and prominent businessmen from Juarez on the other side of the line. They get together at intervals and have a dinner, swap ideas, and make speeches."

"That," Mason said, "is the club I was looking for. I didn't know just where they met."

"They meet here in the hotel."

"Thank you very much," Mason said.

He nodded to Della Street, started toward the elevators.

"That's our baby," he said to Della Street.

Mason got himself oriented, then led the way to the room which Selma Anson was occupying under the name of Helen Ebb, knocked on the door.

For a moment there was no sound from within. Mason knocked again, this time louder.

Selma Anson's voice on the other side of the door sounded frightened. "Who is it?"

"Perry Mason," the lawyer said. "Open up."

She unlocked the door, stood gazing with startled eyes at the lawyer and his secretary.

Mason pushed his way into the room, kicked the door shut behind Della Street as soon as she entered, said to Selma Anson, "What's the idea?"

"I ... I ... I can't tell you."

"You'll tell me," Mason said, "right here and now, or get yourself another lawyer. And if you've done what I think you've done, the other lawyer isn't going to be able to do anything for you except relieve you of money."

"What do you think I've done?"

"I think you're trying to run away."

76

She shook her head. "I'm not running away. I'm just putting on a disappearing act."

"What do you mean by that?"

"I had a talk with someone who is in a position to do me a lot of damage. I reached an agreement, under the terms of which I was to absent myself for a period of time where I couldn't be found and . . ."

Mason interrupted to say, "You were sold a bill of goods. You went to see George Findlay. He told you that he could either make you or break you. That he didn't care what happened as far as your husband's poisoning was concerned; he didn't care what happened to the insurance. That all he wanted was to see that Delane Arlington wasn't led down a rosy path to matrimony.

"He told you that if you'd get out under such circumstances that nobody could trace you, that if you'd get out immediately and stay away for a fixed period of time, and have no communication whatever with Delane Arlington, that he'd be in your corner and help you out of your difficulties. Otherwise, he had something to tell the police that was going to be devastating."

Mason indicated a chair for Della Street, walked over and sat on the edge of the bed, leaving Mrs. Anson to let herself down into a straight-backed chair as though her knees had suddenly buckled.

"How . . . how did you know this?"

"Any lawyer with brains enough to pass the bar examination would have known it," Mason said. "You went to your bank, drew out a bunch of money, then went to see George Findlay, then, still keeping the same taxicab, you went to the airport. You didn't try to take any particular plane to any particular destination. You simply looked around the gates to find a plane that was loading.

"The plane that you found which was loading was headed for El Paso. So, automatically, El Paso became your destination for the first leg of your journey of disappearance.

"You looked over the passengers. You found a young

woman, who looked like a likely customer. You offered her a hundred and fifty dollars over the price of her ticket to give you her ticket and her place in line. You told her that she could take a later plane. She jumped at the chance.

"The woman's name was Helen Ebb. You decided that would be as good an alias as anything.

"You took a taxi from the airport to this hotel. You didn't have any baggage. You probably told the clerk some story about your baggage having been delayed and would be coming in on another plane. You decided that tomorrow morning you'd go to the stores and get yourself a new outfit, and then tomorrow you'd start on the second leg of your journey—Mexico City—South America. You were going to keep your share of the bargain to the letter.

"George Findlay intended to double-cross you right from the start. You hadn't any more than got out of town before Findlay called the police and told them that he thought you were resorting to flight.

"For your information, flight is an evidence of guilt in California. Flight can be introduced as evidence against the defendant in a criminal case.

"You've played right into the hands of your enemies. You've now given the District Attorney a perfect case against you."

"How, in heaven's name, did you know all this?" she asked.

Mason shrugged off the question. "What I want to know is how much money you drew out."

"Sixty thousand dollars."

"Big bills?"

"Hundreds."

"Give me two thousand," Mason said. "You'll never see it again. I'm going to try to buy your way out of this. Della Street will stay with you until I get back. I'll be gone for about twenty minutes to half an hour."

"What are you going to do?"

"I told you I was going to try to buy your way out of this."

78

"Bribery?"

"Don't be foolish," Mason said. "I am an officer of the Court. I have to use the highest standards of ethics. They're having a meeting of the International Exchange Club downstairs. I hope to heaven there's a newspaper reporter there, and I hope he's reasonably smart."

Mason looked at his watch.

"Time's running out," he said. "Give me the two thousand in hundreds."

Selma Anson went to her handbag, opened it. It was bulging with bills. She counted out twenty one-hundred-dollar bills.

"Wait here, Della," Mason said, jerked the door open and disappeared into the corridor.

Selma Anson said to Della Street, "Do you have any idea what he's going to do?"

Della Street shook her head, said, "I think you're going to be interviewed by the press. You don't want to look like this. Get some cold water on your face, then follow through with some makeup. We'll order some drinks sent up from the bar. When Mr. Mason comes back, we'll be all set."

Chapter 10

Mason went to the desk, said to the clerk, "Where's this International Exchange Club banquet taking place?"

"We have a little banquet room off the dining room right through that door, then turn to your left."

"Newspaper coverage?" Mason asked.

"Oh, yes, they had two reporters there. I think one of them has left, but one is still there."

"Thanks," Mason told him, and went through the dining room into the little private banquet hall where some seventy-five people were listening to a speaker who was talking on international goodwill.

Mason stood in a corner of the room until the speaker had finished and was given a round of applause. Then Mason pushed his way up to the microphone at the speaker's table, caught the eye of the toastmaster, and moving toward him, said, "My name is Mason. I'm an attorney from Los Angeles. I tried to get here sooner, but I missed my plane. I have an important message to give to this organization. It will take five minutes."

The toastmaster said, "Mr. *Perry* Mason?"

"That's right."

The man's face lit up. "I've heard of you. It's a real pleasure to meet you."

The man held up his hand for silence, said into the microphone, "Gentlemen, I want to introduce an attorney from Los Angeles, who has an important message for us. I think all of you have heard of Perry Mason, the very famous attorney. Mr. Mason tried to get here earlier, but on account of business problems which detained him in his office, missed his plane and had to take a later plane. He has asked me to apologize to the members of this organization and has assured me that his message will take approximately five minutes."

The speaker turned, extended his hand and said, "Gentlemen, I give you the one and only Perry Mason!"

There was a burst of enthusiastic applause. One man stood up, the others followed, and Perry Mason received a rising ovation.

When the smiling lawyer had the diners seated once more, he said, "Gentlemen, I'm going to be very brief. I have a client, a Los Angeles heiress, who does not wish her identity known. She has taken great precautions to keep anyone from finding out who she is. I may say that she came here traveling under an assumed name. She is my client, and she has asked me to be her spokesman on this occasion.

"My client realizes that more depends upon international friendship than is generally considered the case.

"We are now reaching an age of international cooperation. Force is becoming so destructive that it will soon be outmoded. International friendship and mutual understanding will supplement the narrow-minded selfishness with which nations have tailored their relations in the past.

"My client has made a study of various organizations which are contributing in the full sense of the word to international understanding. She has decided that you gentlemen are promoting the right kind of friendship and harmony.

"In short, gentlemen, my client has requested me to keep her name entirely out of it; to refer to her simply as my client or as Mrs. Anonymous. But she has asked me on her behalf to donate to you tonight the sum of two thousand dollars, to be used as you see fit in any type of publicity or in simply paying some of the expenses of the organization.

"It, therefore, gives me great pleasure to count out twenty one-hundred-dollar bills."

Mason withdrew the sheaf of bills from his inner coat pocket, counted them out one at a time.

For a moment there was stunned silence. Then there was a roar of applause, and once more the audience came to its feet.

Mason smiled, bowed, and left the speaker's table.

"One minute. One minute!" the toastmaster begged. "Mr. Mason, we want to thank you. We want to pass a resolution . . ."

"Don't thank me," Mason said. "Thank Mrs. Anonymous. And if you want to pass a resolution which she can read in the newspapers, I'm certain she will enjoy that, but the knowledge that she has been permitted to participate in some small way in your activities is all the thanks she wants.

"As it happens, however, my client and I have some very important business to discuss in connection with other philanthropic donations and I must go to her."

Mason bowed, waved his hand to the crowd in the banquet room and left amidst a thunderous roar of applause.

The lawyer hesitated for a moment as he entered the lobby of the hotel, looked behind him from the corner of his eye and saw that a man had unostentatiously left the banquet room, was looking at his wristwatch as though he had an appointment to keep.

Mason went to the desk. "Helen Ebb is in fourteen twenty-seven," he said. "Will you give her a ring and tell her that Perry Mason is on his way up?"

The clerk nodded, reached for the telephone.

Mason went up in the elevator, down the corridor to Selma Anson's room, tapped gently on the door, and it was immediately opened.

Mason said, "Quick now, we haven't time to rehearse things. You're going to be interviewed by a newspaper reporter. You're going to be very much annoyed that he has located you. You're going to let me do the talking. You're going to follow my cue.

"You're a wealthy woman from Los Angeles. You're interested in promoting international friendship. You came here tonight for the sole purpose of having me make a donation to the International Exchange Club in your behalf without disclosing your name and . . ."

Knuckles sounded on the door.

Mason moved over to open the door.

A smiling, well-dressed young man in his thirties said, "Mr. Mason?"

Mason let surprise show in his manner and in his voice. "Why, yes!"

"I'm Bill Pickens of the *Chronicle*," the man said, extending his hand.

Mason hesitated a moment, then took the proffered hand. "Pleased to meet you, Mr. Pickens," he said.

"I was down at the Exchange Club," Pickens said, "and I wanted to ask you a few questions. May I come in?"

Mason said, "I would prefer to have you interview me a little later. I . . ."

"I have a deadline to meet," Pickens said, "and it's rather important."

The young man pushed his way into the room, turned to the two women, said, "My name is Pickens. You'll pardon me for interrupting. I'm a reporter with the *Chronicle* and I have a deadline to meet."

Della Street smiled and nodded.

Pickens studied her intently for a moment, then turned to Selma Anson.

"I can understand your desire for anonymity," he said, "but you're registered as Helen Ebb. Is that your true name?"

Mason said, "Now, just a minute! Just a minute! What is this?"

Pickens said, "It's an interview by a newspaper reporter, and I can assure you, Mr. Mason, that I'm going to do everything possible to cooperate with you—if you, in turn, cooperate with me."

Mason said, "This is a development we hadn't anticipated."

Pickens smiled and said, "After all, Mr. Mason, I'm a newsman. I'm on the track of a good story, and, as you probably know, a good story can be sold to the wire services by the local reporters and the money which comes in from that is a very welcome addition to our somewhat meager salaries.

"These meetings of the International Exchange Club are all about the same, a lot of talks along similar lines, a lot of applause, a lot of handshaking, but not much of a story.

"Now, you come in and give us a whale of a story. I can get it from you the easy way, or I can get it through my connections the hard way. If this woman's name is really Helen Ebb, I'll get on the telephone and find out all about her within half an hour. If she's traveling under an assumed name, I want to know her real identity. After all, this is a story with a local angle and it also has a Los Angeles angle. If the story is right, and I think it is right, I can get a sale to the wire service.

"Here's a woman who is interested in international friendship. Her ideas are going to be worth quoting. She has a passion for anonymity. She hires a high-priced attorney to come from Los Angeles to make a presentation in her name."

Pickens turned to Della Street and said, "I presume you're related in some way to Helen Ebb?"

Della Street looked at Perry Mason.

Mason shook his head and said, "This is Della Street, my confidential secretary."

Pickens said, "Now, if you'll introduce me to Helen Ebb, giving me her right name, it will save us all a lot of trouble."

Mason sighed, "All right," he said. "Meet Selma Anson, of Los Angeles. I'm afraid, Mrs. Anson, I was a little clumsy in handling the matter. I didn't realize a newspaper reporter would be covering the banquet . . . The cat is now out of the bag and we may as well accept the situation with good grace."

Selma Anson drew herself up and said, "I fail to see any reason why I should be called on for any statement. After all, Mr. Mason, I retained you to assure me that . . ."

84

"I know. I know," Mason interrupted. "But we are faced with facts, Mrs. Anson, and recrimination is going to do us no good at this point."

Pickens smiled reassuringly. "Mr. Mason is right, Mrs. Anson, and, after all, when it comes to publicity it's a question of the kind of publicity you want. If you want *good* public relations, that's one thing. If you make things difficult for the press and have bad public relations, that's something else again."

"Is this a threat?" she asked.

"Certainly not!" Mason interposed. "Mr. Pickens is simply telling you the facts of life."

Mason turned to the reporter. "I can tell you this, Mr. Pickens, we started out from Los Angeles. Mrs. Anson inherited some money recently and has a list of pet projects which she wants to encourage. She is very much interested in international relations and there are several other charities in which she's interested."

Pickens whipped some folded newsprint from his pocket, took out a soft lead pencil and started scribbling notes.

"What are they?" he asked.

"What are what?" Mason asked.

"The other projects."

Mason shook his head emphatically. "You have penetrated our disguise as far as this donation is concerned, Pickens, but you're not going to be able to make a premature announcement which would destroy the very effect Mrs. Anson is trying to create. In other words, we're not going to give you the names of the other projects."

"Can you tell me how many of them there are?"

Mason said, "You are free to say there are over half a dozen."

"And you intend to give them all a substantial donation?"

"A substantial cash donation."

"And Mrs. Anson wants to have the situation handled so that she will be in the background?"

"So that her identity will never be uncovered," Mason

85

said. "She wants to have me simply appear before the various meetings of these bodies that she wants to encourage and make a donation just as I made a donation to the International Exchange Club tonight."

Pickens said, "Very, very commendable. I can assure you that we appreciate your cooperation. Now, what can you tell me about the background of Mrs. Anson?"

Mason said, "Mrs. Anson is a widow. Her husband died rather suddenly and she received a large sum of money on an insurance policy. I may say that Mrs. Anson is a very good business woman. She invested the funds wisely and has made a substantial increase in the amount of the inheritance."

"I can describe her as a wealthy woman?" Pickens asked.

Mason nodded.

Pickens said, "I think this is wonderful. Can you tell me a little more about how she tried to keep her anonymity? After all, coming to El Paso was pretty much of a giveaway."

"It would have been under ordinary circumstances," Mason said, "but Mrs. Anson played it rather smart. She located a Helen Ebb who was taking a plane to El Paso. She made Helen Ebb a substantial cash bonus in order to take over her ticket and her seat on the plane, and then came here."

"And you?" Pickens asked.

Mason made a little grimace. "Mrs. Anson thought that she could handle the situation by herself and make the donation without its being traced."

Mason turned to Selma Anson and said, "What did you intend to do, Mrs. Anson, get a messenger boy?"

She smiled, "I had plans of my own which I don't care to divulge at the present time, but I think they would have been satisfactory."

Mason said, "As soon as I found out what my client was doing, I realized that she would almost inevitably be courting publicity. So I jumped on a plane and came here to consult with her and tell her how I thought the matter should be handled."

Pickens put the newsprint back in his pocket, shook hands with Mason and said, "It's a great story."

"What's great about it?" Mason asked. "After all, it's simply a question of a charitable donation being made by a wealthy woman."

"What's great about it!" Pickens exclaimed. "Wait until you read the *Chronicle* tomorrow morning. This is good for a by-line and a whale of a story. I'll give you a hint about the headlines right now. PERRY MASON COMES OFF SECOND BEST IN ENCOUNTER WITH CHRONICLE REPORTER."

Mason winced visibly.

"It won't hurt," Pickens said. "Those will be the headlines. The story will be a dilly; and then I'll follow it up with a straight news story about the Helen Ebb angle, and tell the wire services about Selma Anson and her wonderful ideas for improving international relations and how she feels about Mexico and the United States."

"You haven't asked her about that," Mason said.

"I don't need to," Pickens said. "I've got a deadline to meet and two thousand dollars covers a hell of a lot of words. Thank you very much indeed, and good night."

Pickens jerked the door open, turned, gave them a friendly smile and was out in the corridor.

Selma Anson turned to Perry Mason, "Now what?" she asked.

Mason said, "Go to bed. Go to sleep. I'll see you in the morning."

Chapter 11

Mason, carrying a folded newspaper under his arm, strolled into the dining room, glanced at his wristwatch, yawned, and took a seat at a table for two.

"I expect my secretary to join me momentarily," Mason told the waitress. "I telephoned her room and she said she was just about ready for breakfast."

Again the lawyer stretched and yawned.

"Bring me some tomato juice and then a pot of coffee, if you will, please. We'll put the order in, in a few minutes."

The waitress nodded and withdrew.

Mason casually unfolded the newspaper.

A voice at his elbow said, "Well, *this* is a surprise!"

Mason looked up into the shrewd, suspicious eyes of Lieutenant Tragg of the Los Angeles Homicide Division.

"Good heavens!" Mason said. "What are *you* doing here?"

"*I'll* ask the questions," Tragg said. "The first one is, what are *you* doing here?"

"You'll ask the questions?" Mason asked. "What the heck do you think this is, a murder case?"

"Exactly," Tragg said.

"Are you kidding?" Mason asked.

"I was never more serious in my life."

The waitress brought Mason's juice and the pot of coffee.

"Can you draw up another chair for Lieutenant Tragg?" Mason asked. "Or can we move to another table?"

"Don't bother," Tragg said. "I'm over here with one of the detectives from the El Paso Detective Bureau. As soon as I've had breakfast we're going to call on a woman who is here at the hotel and who is, we believe, a fugitive from justice in California."

"*After* breakfast?" Mason asked.

"Exactly," Tragg said. "I had to travel all night to get here and I'm going to have some hot coffee and something in my stomach before I go to work. Sid Russell of the El Paso Detective Bureau met me at the airport and he's had the room we want put under surveillance ever since six o'clock this morning so our quarry can't escape."

Mason said, "I didn't know you had official business here. Under the circumstances, Lieutenant, you really must join me, or perhaps let me join you."

Tragg hesitated. "Perhaps *you'd* better join *us*."

Mason motioned to the waitress, handed her a dollar bill, "Sorry to inconvenience you," he said, "but would you transfer me over to that table for four? Lieutenant Tragg and his friend are there now and when my secretary comes in we'll have the table filled."

"Oh, I'll be glad to," she said, "and thank you!"

Tragg put his hand on Mason's elbow with a firm, almost an official gesture.

"Right this way, Perry," he said.

Tragg led the lawyer over to the table where Tragg's breakfast companion was watching the proceedings with undisguised curiosity.

"Detective Russell," Tragg said, "I want to introduce Perry Mason, a Los Angeles lawyer."

"Not *the* Perry Mason?" Russell said, getting to his feet.

"*The* Perry Mason," Tragg said dryly. "And when he shows up anywhere it usually means trouble for law enforcement. He's going to have breakfast with us and he's going to tell us what he's doing in El Paso."

"Oh, but I can't do that, Lieutenant," Mason protested. "After all, I'm here as an attorney, and I have to protect the confidences of my clients."

"You have a client here?" Tragg asked suspiciously.

Mason smiled, "I'm afraid you're putting words in my

mouth. It's a real pleasure to meet you, Detective Russell. Lieutenant Tragg has been kind enough to invite me to have breakfast over here at this table, and . . . Well, well, well, here's my secretary now. If you'll pardon me for a moment I'll escort her over."

Tragg had no intention of letting Mason exchange any word in confidence with Della Street.

"How nice to see Della here, too!" he exclaimed. "I'll go right over with you, Perry, and greet her."

Tragg marched beside Perry Mason to where Della Street was standing in the doorway, looking around the dining room.

Her eyes lit as she saw Perry Mason, then widened as she saw Lieutenant Tragg.

"Well, well, well, Della!" Tragg said. "Welcome to El Paso."

"Good morning, Lieutenant. Are you stationed here now?"

"Just temporarily on a matter of official business," Tragg said. "A little matter that needs clearing up."

"Someone from Los Angeles is here in the hotel," Mason explained casually. "Someone apparently the lieutenant has an interest in."

"Yes, indeed," Lieutenant Tragg said, "and I'm beginning to think it's a remarkable coincidence finding *you* here, Perry. And, of course, you, Miss Street."

Della Street simply gave him a gracious smile.

"The lieutenant has invited us to have breakfast over at his table," Mason said, and added, "Dutch treat, of course."

"Oh, of course, of course," Tragg said. "The Department doesn't like to have us running around entertaining defense lawyers and their secretaries. It'll be Dutch treat. Unless, of course, you want to pick up the check, Perry."

"I might even do that," Mason said.

The trio walked over to the table, where Mason introduced Detective Russell to Della Street, and then held a chair for Della Street to be seated.

90

The waitress was watching the whole affair with undisguised interest.

Mason finished seating Della Street at the table, smiled at Lieutenant Tragg and said, "You people have ordered?"

"We've ordered," Tragg said, and indicating the big pot of coffee in front of him said, "I had her bring coffee before she even took our order. We've got ham and eggs coming."

"How are you feeling, Della?" Mason asked.

"Fine," she said.

"Feel up to ham and eggs?"

"I want tomato juice to start with," she said, "and then I'm going to have sausage and eggs."

She smiled at Lieutenant Tragg. "When you're traveling with Perry Mason you learn to eat when you can get it."

"In my business," Lieutenant Tragg said, "you learn to eat *if* you can get it."

Detective Russell, obviously impressed by Della Street's well-groomed beauty and the prestige of having breakfast with Mason said, "When you're working on a city police force you learn to eat when you can pay for it. Or, what I should say is, when an officer from another city shows up and tells you he's on an expense account."

There was a little polite laughter.

The waitress brought platters of ham and eggs to Lieutenant Tragg and Sid Russell, took orders from Mason and Della Street and withdrew.

"You folks go right ahead," Mason said. "I'll take a glance at the headlines in the paper and, after you finish eating, we'll visit."

"After we finish eating, we've got to go to work," Tragg said.

"Interview?" Mason asked.

"Interview," Tragg said, laconically.

Mason opened the paper, caught Della Street's eye, gave her a slow wink, turned casually through the pages, suddenly stiffened, "Good heavens!" he said. "The guy really wrote it up the way he said he would."

"What guy?" Tragg asked.

"That newspaper columnist," Mason said. "I guess he's a reporter and a columnist."

"That's the El Paso paper," Russell said.

"That's right," Mason told him, "this man's name is Bill Pickens. Do you know him?"

"Do I know him!" Russell said. "I'll say I know him! He's a thorn in my flesh. The guy is always publishing things—runs a column, does general reporting, and sells stories to the wire services. He's a good man, but too darn competent."

Tragg slowly put down his knife and fork. "He's got something in there about you?" he asked.

"Uh huh," Mason said. "You see we came here very, very hush-hush. That is, we were making a donation to a charitable enterprise on behalf of a client who wishes, above all things, to preserve her anonymity. I'm afraid I made the mistake of underestimating this reporter's ability and he managed to follow me and learn the identity of my client. That ruined everything as far as she was concerned."

Tragg, in an ominously level voice, said, "Did this man, Pickens, by any chance publish the name of your client?"

"He certainly did," Mason said. "It's right here in the article. Selma Anson, a Los Angeles heiress, trying to keep her identity concealed under the name of Helen Ebb so she could make a donation to the International Exchange Club in the interest of better . . ."

"Let *me* see that article," Tragg said abruptly, pushing aside his plate of food and taking the newspaper from Mason.

Tragg read a few lines, then turned so that Russell could read over his shoulder. "Get a load of this," he said.

For some minutes, the two men read, then Tragg sighed, folded the newspaper, handed it back to Mason.

Russell said, "You can't underestimate Bill Pickens."

"Underestimate Pickens, my eye," Tragg said. "Mason isn't *that* stupid. He decoyed Pickens down a garden path."

"This woman, Selma Anson," Russell said, "isn't she the one that . . . ?"

"She's the one," Tragg said wearily.

"I'm afraid I don't get you, Lieutenant," Mason said, refolding the newspaper. "But do go ahead with your breakfast and we'll talk afterwards. I know how hungry you are."

"I *was* hungry," Tragg said. "You'd make any good officer lose his appetite."

"I don't get it," Russell said.

"It's simple," Tragg told him. "This Selma Anson gets in a panic and takes off, using an alias. Mason catches up with her and, by the time he gets done manipulating the facts around, Selma Anson isn't running away from any inquiry, oh, good heavens, no! She's a philanthropist, engaged in promoting international friendship. She's unnaturally modest and she's trying to remain anonymous."

"Anything wrong with that?" Mason asked.

"Lots wrong with it," Tragg said. "If she's trying to remain anonymous, why did she come here to the hotel? Why didn't she simply give you the money?"

"Because," Mason said, "this is only one of a series of charitable gifts which she had planned to make. We were going to leave here and go to other cities and attend other meetings. I was going to keep her in the background, but she wanted to have the satisfaction of hearing of the gratitude of the recipients and having my firsthand reports as to how the gift was received and all that."

Tragg sighed, pulled the platter of ham and eggs over toward him and started eating. "Well, I'll choke it down because I'm going to need the nourishment," he said.

"This alters the situation?" Russell asked.

"This raises hell with the situation!" Tragg exploded. "The woman we want to interview is Mason's client. Mason is here. Our chances of getting anything out of her without Mason being at the interview are nil."

Mason said, "Oh, I'm quite sure she'll tell you all about her charitable donations. Of course, you can't expect her to divulge the identity of the various charities to which she intended to donate. That would completely destroy the element of surprise and would be unfair to my client. But, since the donation to the International Exchange Club has already been publicized, there's no reason why we can't discuss that."

"Then perhaps we can discuss why she took a taxicab to the Los Angeles airport and came here under an assumed name?" Tragg asked.

Mason smiled. "Lieutenant," he said, "you jump to erroneous conclusions. She didn't come here under an assumed name."

"The hell she didn't," Tragg said. "She came here under the name of Helen Ebb."

"That's not an *assumed* name," Mason said. "That's a *borrowed* name. She had to come under the name of Helen Ebb because she purchased Helen Ebb's ticket on the plane. And if she hadn't boarded the plane as Helen Ebb, she couldn't have made the flight."

"And she registered here under the name of Helen Ebb?"

"Of course, she did," Mason said. "She came here under the borrowed name of Helen Ebb and she registered at the hotel under that name. She was trying to preserve her anonymity for the purpose of making a charitable donation."

"And she wasn't trying to avoid being questioned by the Los Angeles Police and resorting to flight?"

"Questioned about what?" Mason asked.

"The murder of her husband."

"Good heavens," Mason said, "are you seriously considering questioning her in connection with her husband's death?"

"Of course, we are."

"Well, you didn't have to come flying to El Paso," Mason said. "All you had to do was to give me a ring and ask me to have my client at the District Attorney's office at any time you mentioned, and I'd have been only too glad to have had her there."

"To answer questions?" Tragg asked.

"Certainly," Mason said. "Of course, there are some

questions which I would advise my client not to answer. Because if you *are* contemplating presenting any charges against her, I certainly don't want to have her waive any of her constitutional rights. When you finish with your breakfast, would you like to go up and visit with Mrs. Anson?"

"With you present, of course," Tragg said.

"Oh, certainly."

"I think," Tragg said, "that might be a waste of time. Let me have the newspaper, if you will, please."

Mason handed over the newspaper.

Tragg took a generous helping of ham and eggs from his plate, then, with his mouth full, spread the paper out and started reading.

For a while, he continued to chew, then, as he concentrated on what he was reading, he forgot to move his jaws until at length he had finished a second careful reading of the story.

Tragg pushed the paper away, washed down the food with a swallow of coffee, sighed and said, "Here we go again. I doubt if anything we can get from Mrs. Anson will be worth the wear and tear on the elevator."

"Mind if I read it again?" Russell asked.

Tragg passed the newspaper over.

The El Paso detective reread the story. A slow smile spread over his face. "Bill Pickens," he said, "seems to have cut himself quite a piece of cake."

"Exactly," Tragg said, "and you notice how easy it was for him. The great criminal attorney comes here from Los Angeles, walks into a meeting where there are newspaper reporters present, pays two thousand dollars to get a front-page story in the paper, and then innocently—oh, *so* innocently—walks out and leaves a broad trail directly to his client who is trying so hard—oh, *so* hard—to remain anonymous."

Russell said, "I never thought of it that way when I was reading what Bill Pickens had to say."

"Well, think of it that way now," Lieutenant Tragg snapped. "If we go up and talk with Mrs. Anson, it will be like seeing a perfectly rehearsed play where the actors are all letter-perfect in their parts. Mason would have made a great director. It was a sorry day for law enforcement when Perry Mason was admitted to the Bar."

"Come, come, Lieutenant," Mason said. "I assist law enforcement. I see that the innocent are acquitted and the guilty are brought to justice. What more can you ask of law enforcement than that?"

"A little more orthodox methods for one thing," Tragg said.

The waitress brought Della Street and Mason their plates and Mason said to her, "Bring me the check for all of this table, if you will, please. That will be my contribution to law enforcement."

Tragg said, "You'll insist on being present at all stages of the interview if we talk with Mrs. Anson, Mason?"

"Certainly."

"Will you let her answer questions?"

"Some questions," Mason said thoughtfully. "Some questions I'll answer for her."

"What questions will you let her answer?"

"If you ask her if she knows anything about the death of her husband which would incriminate her, I will let her answer that question in the negative."

"In other words, you'll stand by with a whitewash brush and put on either one or two coats as the case may be?"

"I didn't say that."

"I'm saying that."

Mason said, "I don't like to keep contradicting you, Lieutenant."

"And after the interview?" Tragg asked.

Mason spread his hands in a gesture of futility. "There's no use trying to go ahead with our anonymous charitable donations now. Thanks to this Bill Pickens, the beans have been spilled and, of course, your story will be a clincher."

"What do you mean my story?"

"Oh, Bill Pickens will want to follow up," Mason said. "And I suppose he's shrewd enough to get it. I saw him look in the restaurant a moment ago. He evidently inquired for me and the clerk told him I was in the restaurant. He'll be waiting to buttonhole me when we come out and, of course, I'll introduce him to you. I take it that he knows Detective Russell—and Pickens will be smart enough to put two and two together even if he doesn't want an exclusive interview with Selma Anson afterwards.

"He has just handed himself a bouquet for getting a story about me that I didn't want published . . . oh, this will be a great day for Bill Pickens."

Tragg said, "*We* don't want any publicity at the moment."

"I see your position," Mason said smilingly.

Tragg sighed. "Okay, Mason, you win this hand. Pay the check. Give the girl a good tip. Forget about Selma Anson. Go ahead and get your newspaper publicity. We won't help you play it up."

Lieutenant Tragg turned to the El Paso detective, "That right, Sid?"

"Right," Russell said.

The waitress appeared. "Everything all right?" she asked.

"It is now," Tragg said. "Give Mr. Mason here the check, and get a good tip because he's just made a good fee."

Chapter 12

Mason tapped gently on the door of Selma Anson's room.

"Who is it?" she called.

"Perry Mason and Della Street."

There was the sound of a bolt being turned and the door opened.

Selma Anson, looking worn and haggard said, "Come in, please."

"Did you have a good night?" Mason asked.

"I had a terrible night," she said, "and my makeup won't cover the ravages."

Mason said, "Lieutenant Tragg of the Los Angeles Police force is here in El Paso. He has a detective from El Paso working with him. There's a chance they may try to work a rush act on you and trap you into some admissions.

"I invited Lieutenant Tragg to come up here with us and question you in my presence. He didn't want any part of that. Now, if he, or anyone else, tries to question you when I am not here, simply state that you have been instructed by your attorney, Mr. Mason, not to answer any questions except in his presence. Can you do that?"

"Oh, I suppose so," she said wearily. "But, Mr. Mason, what is all this going to lead to? What will it do to me?"

"What do you mean?"

She said, "This business of having lawyers and playing games with the police. My life is ruined already. We might as well let them arrest me if they want to and get it over with."

"What do you mean, your life is ruined?" Mason asked.

"Well," she said, "I . . ."

"Go on," Mason said, as she hesitated.

"Well, it's ruined, that's all."

Mason said, "You did your best to ruin your life. You went to see George Findlay. George told you that he knew something that would ruin you. His price for silence was that you get out.

"We all know Findlay's motivation. He intends to marry Mildred Arlington. On her uncle's death, he intends to quit work and take life easy, traveling around the world, living on the money his wife inherits.

"You enter the picture and Delane Arlington starts falling in love. It's rather obvious to anyone who is observing from the sidelines, and it's doubly obvious to someone like Findlay who has interests which will be jeopardized.

"So, Findlay starts scheming, and probably Mildred Arlington, whom he intends to marry, is mixed up in it just as deep as he is.

"Then, they pull this amateur, theatrical stunt of telling you to disappear and never see Mildred's uncle again and they won't ruin your life.

"You fall for it like a little fool."

"What do you mean, like a little fool!" she blazed. "I had everything to gain and nothing to lose."

"What do you mean, nothing to lose?"

"Don't you see, under the circumstances I can never see Delane Arlington again. I can never let his intentions become serious. I can never let him propose to me and I can never, never, never marry him."

"Why?"

"A matter of pride, for one thing. But, by the time they finish poisoning his mind, he'll never propose to me and, if he did and if I accepted, it wouldn't be long before the chorus of hate and suspicion and vicious rumors would poison his mind so he'd never go through with it."

Mason said, "What you don't realize is that you did have a lot to lose. The minute you cleared out, George Findlay tipped the police off, probably by an anonymous telephone call that you had resorted to flight because you were afraid you were going to be convicted of murdering your husband.

And if I hadn't been on the job, you'd have walked right into *that* trap. The Los Angeles police would have picked you up and you'd be in jail right now, charged with murder. For your information, Lieutenant Tragg was here for that very purpose. It was the story in this morning's paper that spiked his guns and left him helpless."

"I'm very, very grateful to you for that," she said.

"You should be," Mason told her.

"What can we do now?" she asked. "What's next?"

Mason turned to Della Street. "See about the air schedules, Della."

Della Street got on the phone.

Mason said, "We're returning to Los Angeles just as soon as we can get transportation."

"Will I be questioned by the press when we arrive?"

"Probably," Mason said.

"What will I tell them?"

"Simply smile," Mason said, "and refer them to me. In fact, from now on don't tell anybody anything unless I tell you to."

She said, "It doesn't make any difference what happens as far as I'm concerned. My life from now on is going to be a treadmill. I didn't realize how deeply in love I was until—until everything was ruined."

"Forget it," Mason told her. "You're not licked yet. Every once in a while we get in a situation where the best defense is a counteroffensive. We are going to initiate a counteroffensive."

"How?" she asked.

"Leave that to me," Mason said. "I just want to know whether you had anything to do with your husband's death—and I want the truth."

"I've already told you, Mr. Mason. I had nothing to do with his death."

"You listen carefully," Mason told her, "if you're telling the truth I think we can pull a fast one on the police and help you. But if you're lying we'd better leave things just as they are."

100

"I'm not lying."

"Look me in the eyes," Mason said.

She gave him a steady unwavering look.

"You understand that if you're lying and are guilty, what I am planning to do will be suicidal?"

"I'm innocent."

"You authorize me to proceed on that assumption?"

"Yes."

"All the way?"

"All the way."

Della Street, from the telephone, said, "There's a plane that leaves in an hour. We can just make it if we hurry."

"We hurry," Mason said. "Thank heavens, there's no packing to do."

"What do you mean, thank heavens," Della Street commented. "Do you realize what it means to take a woman on a plane to a distant city with no makeup except one little compact?"

Mason brushed the comment aside. "I'll check out down at the desk and have a cab waiting."

"Any chance Lieutenant Tragg will be going back on that same plane?" Della Street asked.

"Probably not," Mason said. "He was up all night. He'll want rest and he may want to look around El Paso before he goes back. The police like to entertain visiting colleagues.... We're on our way."

The lawyer checked out the three rooms with the cashier, secured a taxi and was waiting when Della Street and Selma Anson came down in the elevator.

They made it to the airport with time to spare, and settled back on the big jet plane, which lifted them high over the Rio Grande Valley, across the desert, over the fertile Salt River Valley of Arizona, then across more desert until it began its descent, winging over the Coachella Valley, where fertile date palms formed green patches, and then into the crowded, traffic-filled confines of the Los Angeles Basin.

As Mason escorted the two women to the gate a newspaper reporter with a photographer came pushing forward. "Mr. Mason?" he asked.

"Yes?"

"Is this Selma Anson with you?"

"One of the women is, yes."

"Is it true that police have been seeking her to question her in connection with the death of her husband?"

"How would I know?" Mason said. "I can't read the minds of the police, and," he added smiling, "they can't read mine. At least, I hope they can't."

"May we have some pictures?"

"Certainly," Mason said. "Where do you want us?"

"Right over here by the plane, if you don't mind," the photographer said.

Mason, Selma and Della Street followed back through the gates to the steps of the plane and the photographer took a couple of flash pictures with the plane in the background.

"May I ask where you've been?" the reporter asked.

"Certainly," Mason said. "I think there's a story of our trip on the wire services. Mrs. Anson went to El Paso to make an anonymous donation to a group whose work she has followed for some time.

"She made every attempt to remain anonymous, but a clever reporter for the El Paso *Chronicle* penetrated behind the scenes and discovered her identity."

"You weren't interviewed by the El Paso Police?" the reporter asked.

Mason turned to Selma Anson. "Were you interviewed by the police?" he asked.

She shook her head in the negative.

"Well," Mason said, "that's the story."

"I'd like a little more information," the reporter said. "What are you going to do about this story that the police want to interview Selma Anson?"

"Why do they want to interview her?" Mason asked.

The reporter said, "*I* can't read the minds of the police,

but I gather they feel that she has some hitherto undisclosed information abut the death of her husband."

"I'll tell you what I *am* going to do," Mason said. "I'll give you an exclusive story if you have the guts to make a story out of it."

"Try me," the reporter said.

"Mrs. Anson has been pushed around far enough," Mason said. "The Double Indemnity Accident and Life Insurance Company is trying to recover the money which was paid on the death of her husband, William Harper Anson. I understand that insinuations have been made that Mrs. Anson may have poisoned her husband.

"Now, Mrs. Anson is going to take a cab with Miss Street and me.

"Before we get in the cab to start for my office I am going to call Duncan Harris Monroe and ask him to make arrangements to interrogate Mrs. Anson."

"Duncan Harris Monroe?" the reporter said. "You mean the lie detector man?"

"I'm not too keen about that name," Mason said. "I prefer to consider Mr. Monroe as a scientific interrogator. He, of course, uses the polygraph to assist him in reaching his conclusions just as a doctor uses a stethoscope to make his prognosis.

"Unfortunately, the polygraph has been referred to popularly as a lie detector. It is considered by the public to be an instrument that detects the perpetrator of a lie and fastens guilt on him. What the public doesn't know is that the prime purpose of scientific interrogation with the polygraph is, or should be, to establish innocence.

"I am going to establish the innocence of Selma Anson. I'm going to ring up the representative of the Double Indemnity Accident and Life and ask him if he wants to be present."

"But what's the object of all this?" the reporter asked. "You can't ever use this evidence in court."

"I don't have to use it in any California court," Mason said. "I'll leave it to the prosecution to establish its case in

103

court and to prove Selma Anson guilty beyond all reasonable doubt. But in the meantime, as far as the public is concerned, I'll prove that she's innocent of any wrongdoing."

Selma Anson was watching Mason with openmouthed astonishment.

"You mean you're putting all your eggs in one basket?" the reporter asked.

"I'm a damn good judge of eggs," Mason said. "I know an innocent client when I see one."

"You can establish innocence as well as guilt with a polygraph examination?" the reporter asked.

"Of course, you can," Mason said. "The chances of a woman like Mrs. Anson fooling a scientific interrogator who is using all of the modern means to detect deception are virtually nil."

"The police won't buy it," the reporter objected.

"I'm not asking the police to buy it," Mason said, "but I'm going to ask the reading public to buy it and I'm going to give you the story that will make the reading public buy it."

"We never turn down a story," the reporter said. "But there is, of course, some prejudice against publicizing these lie detector tests."

"Don't call them lie detector tests," Mason said. "I have told you we're not trying to detect lies, we're trying to prove innocence and we're going to do it.

"The human body is made so that it reacts to external stimuli. Have you ever attended a nightclub where some clever artist was putting on a humorous act?"

The reporter looked at him with a puzzled expression and said, "Of course, I have, but I don't see the connection."

"What did the audience do?" Mason asked.

"The audience laughed."

"Did you see anyone who wasn't laughing?"

"I didn't look," the reporter said. "I was laughing myself."

"Was anyone with you?"

"My wife."

"What was she doing?"

"She was laughing."

"What is laughter?" Mason asked. "It's evidence of an emotion. You open your mouth. You go ha-ha-ha. Your diaphragm shakes. Your teeth are exposed. Your lips are back. Your shoulders shake."

"What does that have to do with detecting deception?" the reporter asked.

"Simply this. Human beings are all made the same. When something pleases them, they smile. When something makes them sad, they cry. People laugh in a nightclub. They cry at a funeral. We are all human beings. We have human emotions.

"Some people exhibit emotions better than others, but we all have emotions. When you tell a lie, you have certain emotions. The good liar can suppress those emotions so that they're not visible to the naked eye of the beholder. But you can't conceal emotional disturbance, not with a good scientific examiner, aided by the latest in polygraphs, and telling a lie requires mental effort while telling the truth does not."

"The courts frown on having publicity in connection with lie detector tests, confessions and all that sort of thing," the reporter pointed out.

"Exactly," Mason said. "That's when the polygraph is used to establish guilt. And I wish you'd quit using that word, lie detector. This is going to be a scientific examination to determine innocence and if you don't want this story, just say so, because I presume there are other papers who . . ."

"Don't want this story!" the reporter exclaimed. "Good Lord, man, this is a scoop, a beat, a whale of a story! I just want to be sure I get all the facts right, and I'm baiting you about the polygraph and your belief in the polygraph examination so I can make copy."

"It's not a polygraph examination," Mason said. "It's a

scientific interrogation where the interrogator uses a polygraph.

"There has been altogether too much of the wrong kind of publicity about these examinations. Police use them to determine guilt. Some smart newspaper reporter dubbed the polygraph the lie detector when it first came out and the name has stuck.

"There isn't any such thing as a lie detector. The polygraph is a very delicate machine which registers galvanic skin resistance rate and amplitude of the heartbeat, blood pressure, respiration—in short, emotional disturbance.

"What I'm doing is establishing Selma Anson's innocence. I'm going to have it so she can hold up her head in society and live down all these innuendoes that have been made."

"But suppose the test shows she's guilty?" the reporter asked.

"Then you have a story," Mason said.

"No, I haven't," the reporter said dubiously. "I believe the courts are frowning on publicizing confessions of guilt by the aid of a lie detector. You might be doing something very, very clever, you know."

"What do you mean?" Mason asked.

"If the test shows Selma Anson is innocent, you're going to be sitting on top of the heap. If that test shows she's guilty, and we publish it you are going to be in a position to demand at least a change of venue and . . ."

Mason said, "We're simply going to give my client a scientific interrogation of her interest in the case, her good faith, and then if anybody wants to question the results of that interrogation, I'm going to invite that person to take a test before Monroe to determine his or her good faith, whether the innuendoes and accusations have been made in good faith."

"Oh, oh," the reporter said, and then added after a moment, "when do we start all this?"

"Right away," Mason said.

106

The reporter turned to the photographer. "Plenty of films and flashbulbs?"

"Plenty. This is a Strobe that's good for a hundred pictures."

"You may need them," the reporter said. "Trust Perry Mason to do the spectacular."

Chapter 13

At the office of Duncan Harris Monroe, Mason performed introductions, then said, "Selma Anson was married to William Harper Anson, who died leaving an insurance policy. People have been making a lot of insinuations and innuendoes, and the Double Indemnity Accident and Life Insurance Company investigated the death. An order was issued for the exhumation of the body. The indications are, I understand, that there is arsenic present in sufficient quantities to have caused death. At least, that is what the police are going to claim, and what the insurance company, undoubtedly, will claim.

"I don't care about using the polygraph as an instrument for determining guilt. That's not in my department. However, I have the greatest respect for it as an instrument to determine innocence. I think my client is innocent. I want you to find out."

The photographer popped flashbulbs as Mason made his statement.

Monroe said, "Why come to me?"

"Because you're a member of the American Polygraph Association. You're a college graduate. You have a degree in psychology. You have ten years' experience in scientific interrogation and, among the members of the profession, you have a reputation for being tops.

"Now then, do you want to go ahead, or not?"

Monroe thought the matter over. "This is going to be publicized," he objected.

"You're damn right. This is going to be publicized, win, lose, or draw," Mason told him.

"And you want me to publicize my findings?"

"This newspaper reporter is going to be sitting right here," Mason said. "When you make your report, he's going to take it down."

Monroe shook his head. "I'd have to have all kinds of releases on a deal of that sort," he said.

"You bring out your releases," Mason said. "We'll sign them. We'll all sign them."

"This is most unusual," Monroe objected.

"Who the hell said you had to do everything in the usual manner?" Mason asked. "This woman's life is being ruined by insinuations and the publication of half-truths. We're going to see that the whole truth is published."

"Suppose the test shows that she is not telling the truth?"

"Then, you so report," Mason said. "If you have the interests of your profession at heart, I think you will agree with me that one of the greatest uses of the polygraph examination is to establish innocence.

"I can cite at least one national instance, in the Sam Sheppard case. There were whispers going around that the members of the family were not and had not been acting in good faith, that they had been on the scene before the police arrived, and had wiped off fingerprints. Though why anyone would have tried to wipe off fingerprints of Sam Sheppard is more than I know. Sam Sheppard was the one man who was entitled to have his fingerprints all over the house.

"All right," Mason went on, "what happened?

"Arrangements were made for both of Dr. Sam Sheppard's brothers and their wives to be examined by a team of the most efficient, the best-known, the most respected scientific interrogators in the country, using the polygraph to assist them in reaching their conclusions.

"The chances that any one of the individuals could have fooled any one of those four experts were negligible. The chances that all four of the people who were examined could have fooled all the examiners were so astronomical as to be rejected from consideration.

"The examination showed all of those four people had

109

acted in good faith, that they had never heard Dr. Sam Sheppard make any statement indicative of guilt. Those results were publicized and the members of the family were once more able to hold up their heads.

"Now, that's exactly what I'm doing in this case. I'm going to have you interview Selma Anson and report what you find. If she's lying, I want you to report it. If she's telling the truth, I want you to report that. I am so convinced she's telling the truth that I'm putting my pile of chips right in the middle of the table."

Monroe turned to Mrs. Anson. "Does all of this meet with your approval, Mrs. Anson?" he asked.

"Why, I . . . this is all completely unexpected . . . I . . . yes. It meets with my approval."

Monroe said, "Mrs. Anson, I'm going to warn you. My scientific examinations are unbelievably penetrating. The instruments I use are exceedingly delicate. If you have any reservations whatever, if there is anything you are trying to conceal, I ask you professionally to leave this office right now and not go any further with the examination."

"Are you trying to frighten me?" she asked.

"I'm trying to tell you the truth."

"And *I'm* trying to tell *you* the truth," she said, defiantly. "You just go ahead with the test."

"If you gentlemen will be seated," Monroe said, "I want to have a private interview with Mrs. Anson and then, after I have uncovered enough of the facts of the case and established rapport with my client, I will proceed with the test.

"Just be seated and make yourselves comfortable."

Again, there were flashbulbs.

The newspaper reporter picked up the telephone, got through to his paper, and started telling the story to a rewrite man.

Mason caught Della Street's eye, gave her a quick wink.

"*I'll* say you're putting on a counteroffensive," she said.

"There's just one thing that bothers me," Mason confessed.

"What's that?" Della Street asked.

"If the police get wise to what we're doing," Mason said, "they'll be ready to arrest Selma Anson before the newspaper can publish the result of the test. Then they'll get a court order restraining the newspapers from giving the result of the test any publicity."

"Can they do that?"

"It's a question," Mason said. "We're exploring an entirely new field of what can be done and what can't be done in the way of publicity. Undoubtedly if the test showed that she was lying and had a guilty knowledge of the death of her husband, she could fire me, get another attorney and that attorney could claim irreparable damage if the result was publicized and probably get a restraining order or a change of venue or perhaps get the judge to warn the newspaper that it would be guilty of contempt of court if it publicized the result of the test."

"And if it shows she's innocent?"

"What right has any court anywhere to tell a citizen that he can't establish his innocence by any way he sees fit when a lot of innuendoes have been used to accuse him of guilt?"

Della Street thought that over.

Mason moved over to join the reporter, who had now hung up the telephone.

"Any further facts you want?" Mason asked.

"Good Lord, yes, keep talking," the reporter said. "This is one whale of a story. The more you stop to think of it the bigger it gets."

"My client is acting within her rights," Mason said.

"But are you, as an officer of the court, within your rights in . . . ?"

"In proving my client's innocence of any crime?" Mason asked. "What the hell kind of a muzzle do you think is being put on the conscientious attorney? No one's going to keep me from doing what I think is for the best interest of my client."

"But," the reporter said, "having the press there and . . ."

"Want to withdraw?" Mason asked.

The reporter merely grinned, drew up his chair beside Mason, said, "Start giving me facts."

Mason gave a concise statement of facts, eliminating from his statement all the confidential matters which his client had told him, giving only information which could have been obtained from the record.

"Aren't you kind of holding out on me?" the reporter asked.

"Of course, I'm holding out on you," Mason said. "I'm giving you the facts that you can get from the records. I can't give you the facts that my client has given me and I can't try to prejudice you."

"I'd like to have a little more background," the reporter said.

Mason told him, "You're getting your story handed to you on a silver platter. Don't start looking for smudges on the platter."

"I won't," the reporter said, laughing nervously.

The door from the inner office opened and Monroe came out.

"Gentlemen," he said, "I'm about to proceed with the examination. I have had a very interesting talk with Mrs. Anson. I think I understand her position and I have every reason to believe she'll be a good subject for a scientific interrogation.

"Now, I have an inner office here which is equipped with electronic devices so that you can hear everything that is being said in the examination room and watch everything that is being done through a one-way mirror.

"I have explained to Mrs. Anson about this office. I have told her that I want at least her attorney to watch the test and have asked her if she has any objection to Miss Street and the other two gentlemen being present. She has signed a written consent that she is perfectly willing to have this done. If you will go through that door to the right, you will find chairs in there and a one-way mirror. I would like to have you watch the examination and listen to what is being said and I want to point out to Mr. Mason that if, at any

112

time, he feels that the best interests of his client are being jeopardized, he is at perfect liberty to press a stop button which is by the chair where he will be sitting and which is labeled STOP BUTTON. The minute he presses that button the examination will cease."

"Good enough," Mason said.

They filed into the observation room. Monroe indicated the chairs they were to occupy and closed the door.

In the adjoining office, through the one-way mirror, they could see Selma Anson seated, apparently at ease, with one of the latest model polygraphs connected so that her respiration, blood pressure, pulse and galvanic skin resistance were ready to be registered on a chart which moved at a regularly timed rate through the polygraph, the rulings on the chart showing the elapsed time in seconds.

Monroe took his seat.

"Are you ready for the questions, Mrs. Anson? Please don't turn your head. Please don't make any motion whatever. Sit entirely motionless. Be calm and relaxed."

"I am ready for the questions."

Monroe kept his voice in a uniform monotone, being careful not to emphasize any words or ideas, doing nothing which would cause any distraction on the part of the subject.

"Is your name Selma Anson?" he asked.

"Yes."

"Do you listen to the radio?"

"Yes."

"Do you intend to lie to me on questions regarding your husband's death?"

"No."

"Did you fly here from El Paso this morning?"

"Yes."

"Do you know who caused your husband's death?"

"No."

"Have you told your attorney the complete truth?"

"Yes."

"Did you ever administer any poison to your husband?"

113

"No."

"Do you ever watch television?"

"Yes."

"Was the poison administered to your husband ever in your possession?"

"No."

"Were you in El Paso last night?"

"Yes."

"Have you lied in answering any question on this test pertaining to your husband's death?"

"No."

Monroe, speaking in the same monotone, said, "I will wait a few minutes, Mrs. Anson, then I will ask these same questions over again. Just kindly relax, please, and refrain from any unnecessary motion."

After a few moments Monroe went through the questions again, then asked them a third time. At the close of the third period of questions, he asked Mrs. Anson, "Have you lied to me in answering any of these questions?"

"No," she said.

"Have you done anything to try to impair the value of these tests?"

"No."

"Have you resorted to any subterfuge or reservations in answering the questions?"

"No."

"That," Monroe announced, "concludes the examination."

He got up from behind the desk, pulled out the long strip of paper from the polygraph, tore it off, unfastened the attachments to Mrs. Anson's body, said, "Would you like to go out to the other room and rejoin your companions, Mrs. Anson? I'll be out in a minute."

Mason nodded to the others. They opened the door from the room where the concealed witnesses could observe what was going on and joined Mrs. Anson in the outer room.

"How did I do?" Mrs. Anson asked Perry Mason.

"Apparently all right," Mason said. "Your voice and manner were consistently steady throughout."

"Then, if the examination is any good," she asked, "he'll certify that I was telling the truth?"

Mason nodded.

The reporter turned to the photographer, who snapped another picture. Then the door opened and Monroe came out, carrying the folded chart of the polygraph.

Again the photographer took a picture.

"Well?" Mason asked.

"In my opinion," Monroe said, "this woman is telling the truth."

The reporter made a dash for the door, followed by the photographer.

Mason shook hands, paid Monroe for the examination, said to Selma Anson, "Go home and forget the whole business, Mrs. Anson. Don't answer any questions asked by anybody. Come on, Della, I think we're due for a bite of lunch."

Chapter 14

Della Street had the newspapers on Mason's desk when he entered the office.

Headlines across the front page read WIDOW EXONERATED. Down below that in slightly smaller type appeared MASON'S CLIENT TAKES LIE DETECTOR TEST.

"How did our reporter handle it, Della?"

"Boy, did he handle it!" Della Street said. "You gave him a story and he really spread it out. He's got a lot of stuff on the history of the polygraph, when it was invented, all about the late Leonarde Keeler, about the American Polygraph Association, and a telephone interview with its president. He really poured it on."

"Any reactions?" Mason asked.

"None so far," Della Street said, "but it's early. The . . ."

The telephone rang. Della Street picked up the instrument, said, "Yes, Gertie," to the switchboard operator, then turned to Mason with a smile, "Hamilton Burger, the District Attorney, is on the line. He wants to speak with you personally."

Mason said to Della Street, "Tell Gertie to put him on."

He picked up the telephone, said, "Yes, Hamilton. Good morning. How's everything this morning?"

"What the hell are you trying to do with all this publicity in that Anson case?" Burger asked.

"Counteract publicity given by the police that Selma Anson had left town so she couldn't be questioned."

"You could have let the police question her."

"Would the police have announced to the press that they considered her innocent?"

116

"They don't consider her innocent and neither does my office, no matter how many lie detector tests you take."

"Come, come, Hamilton," Mason said, "don't refer to it as a lie detector test. It actually isn't. It's a scientific interrogation accompanied by the use of a polygraph."

"All right, all right," Burger said, "very clever. But I call your attention to the fact that the courts are frowning upon the use of publicity of this sort."

"Of what sort?"

"Showing the results of a lie detector test."

"I didn't know that anyone had ever used it to establish innocence," Mason said. "When it's been used, it's usually been used by the police to establish guilt. When they don't get a confession, they call the test inconclusive and let it go at that.

"I'm starting something new. When there has been publicity concerning a case, I think the proper move is for the suspect to submit to scientific interrogation with the aid of a polygraph, and give the public the results."

"The courts won't let you do it," Burger said.

"What court is going to stop me?"

"You'll see. You'll be cited for contempt of court in connection with this last stunt of yours."

"In other words," Mason said, "the courts are going to stop a person from proclaiming his innocence to the world?"

"In this manner, yes."

"Why?"

"The courts won't allow you to use a polygraph test to show that a suspect is guilty."

"All right," Mason said. "How about a confession? Will they permit the publication of a confession?"

"No more," Burger said. "After a defendant has been arrested, if he confesses, the police won't allow that confession to be publicized."

"All right," Mason said, "now let's take the opposite end of the picture. Suppose the suspect declares he's innocent.

117

Are the courts going to prevent him from stating to the public that he is innocent?"

"Certainly not."

"That's the situation in this case," Mason said. "The court could have prevented the publication of a polygraph test showing guilt after a person had been arrested. In this case, the person hasn't been arrested. A person submits to scientific interrogation with the aid of a polygraph.

"We have thought too much about using these scientific tests to show guilt and not enough about using them to establish innocence. A person whose reputation has been smeared by an innuendo or an outright accusation has a right to have that reputation cleared."

"You haven't heard the last of this," Burger blustered, "and I may say that at the proper time and at the proper place I'm going to ask the court to take action."

"What court?"

"The court in which Selma Anson is being tried."

"Is she going to be tried?" Mason asked.

"We have some evidence which we're evaluating at the present time," Burger said. "I believe it is quite likely that she will be tried, despite the very obvious grandstand, flamboyant publicity which you have injected into the case."

"Do you intend to make a statement to that effect to the press?"

"I have already given the press the position of my office in a dignified manner consistent with the administration of justice."

"In other words, you've tried to counteract my publicity," Mason said.

"Not at all. I have been asked to define the position of my office and I have defined it."

"When we get to court," Mason said, "I'll take a look at that statement and see if I consider there's anything in it designed to unfairly influence the public."

"You'll be in a sweet position to do that," Burger said, "after all that blast of publicity on behalf of the defendant in the paper."

Mason said, "A person is always presumed innocent until he's proven guilty, Burger."

Burger said, sarcastically, "Thank you for giving me an opportunity to brush up on fundamental criminal law, Mr. Mason."

"Not at all," Mason said cheerfully. "It's my pleasure. Call me anytime when you want to know anything."

Burger slammed the telephone at his end of the line.

Mason smiled at Della Street.

"Burger says he's given a statement to the press."

"It hasn't been published yet."

"It'll be in the afternoon editions," Mason told her.

Again the telephone rang. Della Street said, "Yes, Gertie," then turned to Perry Mason. "George Findlay is in the outer office. He seems terribly angry and he demands to see you."

"Demands?" Mason asked.

"That's what Gertie said, demands."

"By all means," Mason said, "let's let the demand be acceded to. Tell him to come right in."

Della Street was apprehensive. "Chief, he's angry. Don't you think you'd better ask Paul Drake to step down here and . . ."

"If he makes a pass at me," Mason said, "I'll break his damned neck."

Della Street hesitated a moment, then resignedly went to the door of the outer office and held it open. "You may come in, Mr. Findlay," she said.

George Findlay, a vigorous, broad-shouldered individual of twenty-eight, came storming into the office. "What the hell are you trying to do?" he asked Perry Mason.

Mason regarded the man with calm contemplation. "I'm trying to find out just what it is you want," he said. "I usually don't see people without an appointment, but I made an exception in your case because you seem to be upset. Now, what is it you want?"

"You're mixing into a family affair," Findlay said.

"Sit down," Mason invited. "Tell me why I shouldn't

mix into family affairs. Lawyers quite frequently do, you know."

"This situation is different," Findlay said. "This woman is a scheming adventuress. She's a woman who has already killed one husband, and if she ever gets Uncle Dee in her clutches she'll murder him just as sure as you're sitting there. Uncle Dee wouldn't last two years."

"You're prepared to prove all this?" Mason asked.

"You're damn right I'm prepared to prove it."

"Then you shouldn't waste time talking to me," Mason said. "You'd better see the District Attorney."

"That," Findlay said, "is what I wanted to see you about."

"Indeed!" Mason said. "You're here. Go right ahead. Tell me what it is that's on your mind."

"You're representing Selma Anson," Findlay said. "Now I'm not concerned with Selma Anson. I don't give a damn if she murders twenty husbands just so she keeps her clutches off of Uncle Dee.

"Uncle Dee is a sweet, lovable character who hasn't the faintest idea of the types of people there are in the world, especially the Selma Anson type. He takes everyone at face value. He's taking her at face value.

"Now, I gave Selma Anson one opportunity to call everything off. I understood she took it, but then you entered the picture and upset everything."

"How did I upset it?"

"With that damned lie detector test."

Mason smiled. "That wasn't a damned lie detector test, as you call it," he said. "It was a truth detector test. I wanted to establish the fact that my client was telling the truth."

"I don't know what you were trying to accomplish," Findlay said, "and I don't give a damn. That lie detector evidence isn't going to be admissible in court."

"Please," Mason said, "I repeat. It *wasn't* a lie detector test. I had my client submit to expert interrogation and the

120

interrogator used a polygraph just as a doctor might use a stethoscope."

"But you know it isn't going to be admissible in court."

"I'm not trying to get it admitted in court," Mason said. "My client isn't before the court."

"Well, she will be."

"What do you mean by that?"

Findlay said, "I tried to cooperate with your client, Mason. I'm going to put my cards on the table with you and if you ever try to cross-examine me about this interview, or as to what I said, I'll swear that you're a liar. Now, just have your secretary leave the room and we'll talk man to man."

Mason shook his head. "Talk man to man all you please, but my secretary stays here. If you have anything to say that you don't want brought out in the record, you'd better leave the room before you start talking."

"Now, wait a minute," Findlay said, "we aren't getting anywhere, talking like this."

"Do we have to get somewhere?" Mason asked.

"I think we do."

"Why?"

"Because I can aid your client."

"In what way?"

Findlay said, "I'm not going to put my cards on the table face up until I know what you're holding in your hand."

Mason said, "My position is very simple. I'm representing Selma Anson. There have been intimations made that she knew something about the death of her husband which she has been concealing. Intimations have been made that she may have had something to do with administering poison to her husband. Those intimations and insinuations are slanderous and constitute defamation of character. When I find out just who made them, where they were made, when they were made and to whom they were made, I intend to do something about it."

"You aren't going to frighten me by threats."

"I'm not making threats. I'm making statements."

"I regard them as threats."

"I can't control your thinking, and I don't intend to try."

"You want to protect your client's interest, don't you?"

"I want to protect my client's interests."

"I can be of considerable value along those lines."

"What do you mean by the word, value?"

"I'm not after any money."

"What do you want?"

"Mr. Mason, let's understand each other. I'd like to have you understand my position."

"What is your position?"

"In one way, you might describe me as a friend of the Arlington family."

"That's one way of describing you?" Mason asked.

"Yes."

"Are there others?"

Findlay said, "I presume there are."

"How do you describe yourself?"

"I'm a businessman."

"Go ahead."

"Delane Arlington—Uncle Dee—is a wonderful man."

"No argument."

"Like all mortal flesh he keeps getting older every day he lives."

"No argument."

"He has reached an age when he is lonely and, for that reason, rather susceptible. Your client comes along and impresses him. We all know that when men get hypnotized by sex they lose their sense of values."

"You, yourself, are immune from sex?" Mason asked.

Findlay laughed, "All right, I'm interested in Mildred Arlington. We're going to be married."

"And as such," Mason said, "you're very much interested in seeing that the money from her Uncle Delane comes to her, or at least a large chunk of that money comes to her?"

"Put it that way if you want to."

"I'm just asking," Mason said.

"All right, we're putting cards on the table, that's right."

"Keep talking," Mason told him.

"Now then, your client, Selma Anson, is, as far as you're concerned, a client. You can't see any of her weaknesses. You take her at face value. That's your privilege. That's your duty. But here are the facts. Selma Anson murdered her husband, Bill Anson, in order to get his insurance money. She's done a good thing with that insurance money. She's ambitious, avaricious and smart. She wants to add more money to what she has. She wants to marry Delane Arlington. Once she marries him and gets him to make a will in her favor, Delane Arlington won't last twelve months.

"Selma is a shrewd, clever, resourceful opportunist."

"How about yourself?" Mason asked.

Findlay said, "All right, I am shrewd, clever, resourceful and an opportunist."

"Go on," Mason said.

"The District Attorney would like to convict Selma Anson of the murder of her husband. The insurance company would like very much to have it established that Selma Anson murdered her husband, and, therefore, was not entitled to keep the insurance money, but has been holding it in trust for the insurance company.

"I'm in a position to give the insurance company the evidence it wants and to give the District Attorney the evidence that he wants."

"No comment," Mason said.

"Now, I know that as a lawyer you can't make any kind of a deal. As a witness, I can't make any kind of a deal. But, I don't want to go running around being a stool pigeon for the officers. I don't want to make trouble for Selma Anson. She's a very nice, estimable woman, except for certain traits she has and—well, after all, who am I to sit in judgment."

"Go on," Mason said.

"Now then, if I have to, I can see that Selma Anson doesn't marry Delane Arlington by the simple expedient

123

of having her convicted of murder. That would suit my purposes very well.

"If, on the other hand, Selma Anson voluntarily renounced Delane Arlington, that is, if she went away somewhere, I don't think the District Attorney has enough evidence to convict Selma Anson—at least, he doesn't stand nearly as good a chance of getting a conviction as would be the case if I told him what I know."

"No comment," Mason said.

"I think at this time you should make a comment."

"All right," Mason said, "I'll make a comment. Out!"

"What do you mean? The deal is out?"

"I mean *you're* out," Mason said, getting to his feet, and opening the exit door.

"Now, wait a minute," Findlay said, "you can't brush me off like that. Remember, you have a duty to your client. You are obligated to make any deal which is to her advantage. I'm offering you something that . . ."

"Out!" Mason interrupted.

Findlay got to his feet, "I tell you that . . ."

Mason made a threatening step forward. "Out!"

Findlay caught the look in the lawyer's eyes, turned, started for the exit door. "You'll regret this as long as you live," he said.

"Out!" Mason said.

Findlay said, "You've now forced me to play my trump card."

"In about two seconds," Mason said, moving forward, "you're going to force *me* to play *my* trump card."

Findlay hastily retreated through the door to the corridor.

Mason closed the door.

"Well?" Della Street asked, "do you think he was bluffing?"

Mason shook his head. "I think within twenty-four hours Selma Anson will be arrested for the murder of her husband."

"What do you suppose Findlay has, some definite evidence?"

Mason nodded thoughtfully. "He wouldn't have come to me unless he did have. He was prepared to disclose the nature of his evidence if I'd have given him a chance."

"And you didn't want to give him a chance?"

"We don't deal with that class of citizen," Mason said. "I have a duty to my client and I also have a duty to my profession and to myself."

"I thought you were going to hit him."

Mason sighed. "I thought I was, too," he said. "If I had hit him I'd probably have regretted it for a year."

"But since you didn't?" she asked.

"I'll regret it as long as I live," Mason snapped.

Chapter 15

When Mason entered the office the next morning Della Street looked up, smiled a greeting, and said, "Daphne Arlington is waiting to see you. She's been here ever since the office opened. She was waiting in the hall for Gertie to open up."

"Any idea what it's about?" Mason asked. "This Arlington situation is getting a little complicated."

"She's all worked up about something. I think she would tell me all right, but she didn't want to talk in front of Gertie."

"She's a sweet kid," Mason said. "Have her come in."

Della Street nodded, went to the outer office and returned with Daphne Arlington.

"I'm sorry you were kept waiting, Daphne," Mason said, "but I was delayed a bit this morning."

"It's all right, Mr. Mason. I just wanted to be sure to see you before—well, before anything happened."

"Such as what?" Mason asked.

"It's all so complicated," she said. "I hardly know where to begin, but it has to do with George Findlay and, of course, Mildred, because George has Mildred completely hypnotized. He dominates her thinking."

"Quite a forceful man, I would say," Mason said.

"Forceful and unscrupulous. He's primarily responsible for my coming here."

Mason's eyes narrowed slightly. "You mean he wants you to intercede with me on behalf of . . ."

"No, no, no. Don't get me wrong, Mr. Mason. I do want Uncle Dee to be happy, and I just happen to think that Selma Anson is the woman for him.

"I know it will make a lot of difference financially to me, that is, I think it will, but nevertheless I would like to see them get married. I suppose that's all off now."

"Why?"

"Selma Anson would never consent to marriage as long as this cloud is hanging over her head and this cloud is, I'm afraid, going to hang over her head as long as she lives."

"What about your uncle?"

"Uncle Dee feels even more interested now than ever. He has an idea that he'd like to protect Selma in every way he could and I think he'd propose marriage in a minute—in fact, I think he has."

"But Selma will have none of it?"

"Put yourself in her place, Mr. Mason. There has been this newspaper publicity, all of this gossip in the circles in which she would have to move as Delane Arlington's wife. She has the cold, bitter hostility of most of the family.

"She couldn't face that; the marriage couldn't face that. Uncle Dee couldn't face that. It would mean changing his entire outlook on life. And suppose he gets just a touch of intestinal influenza—you know what would happen. Immediately a whole procession of nephews and nieces would come to his door, saying, 'Uncle Dee, I don't care what *you* think is the matter, but I'm going to have you treated for arsenic poisoning right now.' "

Mason was thoughtfully silent.

"Now," Daphne said, "we come to the reason I'm here so early this morning and the reason I'm so excited.

"I know that George Findlay came to see you, and I think he rather felt he could make some kind of a deal with you. He feels that if Selma Anson would agree, with your consent, to take a trip around the world somewhere, or go some place where Uncle Dee wouldn't have any chance to get in touch with her, and if George kept quiet about some evidence he knows about, the affair would gradually die on the vine.

"Apparently, you turned him down cold and hard.

"Now then, yesterday I walked into the living room for

127

a book I'd left. I'd been playing tennis, and was wearing tennis shoes, so I didn't make any noise when I walked into the room.

"I wasn't eavesdropping because I had no idea anyone was in the room at the time, but Mildred and George Findlay were sitting in a huddle and they seemed to have just reached some decision and were going over the plans. I heard George say, 'And we'll let your uncle discover the evidence that . . .' Then Mildred saw me and kicked George lightly in the shin.

"George got the signal. He didn't even turn around, but hesitated a moment and then went on to say, '. . . the evidence that will show this financial investment would be a waste of money. It will be better to convince him that way than to try to talk with him.'

"Mildred said, 'Yes, I think so, too.' Then looked up and said, 'Was there something, Daphne?'

"I said, 'Just getting a book,' and went out. But I'm satisfied, Mr. Mason, that they were planning some bit of skulduggery. I think they're going to plant some piece of evidence where Uncle Dee will discover it and—well, you can see what will happen, under those circumstances. Uncle Dee would have to report finding the evidence to the police. The police would, in turn, use Uncle Dee as a witness. He would be an unwilling witness, but Uncle Dee would tell the truth no matter what the circumstances.

"If his testimony should send Selma Anson to prison or . . . or . . . or, let's face it, to the gas chamber, you can see what would happen. It would be playing right into Mildred's hands, and, of course, Mildred and George are just the same as one these days."

"They're going to get married?" Mason asked.

"Yes. Sometimes I think they already are married. I think they may have been secretly married, but they're playing things pretty cozy. Uncle Dee doesn't like George. He doesn't like the idea of Mildred marrying him or having George in the family, but Uncle Dee is very tolerant in most respects and he's letting the situation work itself out. That is, he thinks he is.

"Actually, I think Mildred feels that if she married George at the present time, moved out of the house and went to live with George, Uncle Dee—well, he might be prejudiced against George and in favor of the others.

"And she knows that if she married George and had George come to live in the house with the rest of us, there would be friction all over the place."

"Just who is living in the house?" Mason asked.

"Well, I am, of course. And then there's Fowler and Lolita. Fowler is my older brother.

"We all three live in the house. Then, in addition to that, I have another brother just a year older than I am, Marvin Arlington, who is married and lives in San Francisco. We don't see him very often, although he gets together for family days when he can, but his wife, Rosemary, likes to have Thanksgiving with her mother and father. They have no children as yet. They've been married only a little over a year.

"Then, of course, there's Mildred who lives in the house."

"It's a big house?" Mason asked.

"It's an absolutely tremendous house with too many rooms to take care of and too much ground.

"We help with the housework some. There's a housekeeper who comes in, and a cook who comes in. They work by the day and it's pretty hard to keep them. Domestic help is a problem these days."

"Big grounds?"

"I'll say. There's a tennis court, a swimming pool, a summer house, a barbecue arbor—just a big, old-fashioned rambling structure, but it suits Uncle Dee and he likes to have us with him."

"And I take it he's wealthy?" Mason asked.

"Very wealthy."

"He likes to entertain?"

"He did," Daphne said, "but it's getting so now that it's

such a problem with help that he doesn't do things the way he used to. We used to have lots of barbecues. There's a big, long arbor with a table and all the facilities for outdoor cooking. Uncle Dee loved to barbecue steaks. He has a way of cooking them and he has a secret sauce and—well, you know how men are that way."

Della Street smiled. "He knows," she said.

"You feel some evidence might be fabricated?" Mason asked.

"I don't know. All I know is that my cousin Mildred is just as shrewd and just as selfish as they come. And George Findlay is, in my opinion, just a cheap chiseler, a man who would take advantage of anybody in order to accomplish what he wants to accomplish and to get what he wants."

"This dinner where William Anson was poisoned," Mason said, "took place at your uncle's house?"

"Yes, it was a family barbecue, but Selma Anson and her husband were invited. I believe there was some sort of a real estate deal pending. It was a warm night and Uncle Dee was in great form. He was barbecuing the steaks and he had marinated them in his special secret sauce. Lolita had made the salad, and Uncle Dee is particularly fond of her crab salad.

"Lolita had made the salad earlier in the day and had put it in the refrigerator. She took the salad out in order to put some other food in there. She intended to make room and put the salad back but she had a phone call and then had to race to the beauty shop. She had the salad covered so flies couldn't get into it, but it *was* a warm day and I think she left the salad out of the refrigerator all afternoon—but she denies this."

Mason said, "They'll have the deuce of a time showing that Anson's death was due to arsenic poisoning with a case history like that. . . . The dinner took place down there in the arbor?"

"Oh yes, we have the barbecue grate down there and long tables with benches and everything is all fixed up with electric lights, running water; even a little bar and a kitchen."

"And everybody got sick?"

"The people who ate the crab salad had a little trouble. Uncle Dee had quite a bit of trouble. And, of course, poor Mr. Anson was so ill they had to take him to a hospital, and he died there."

"No one suspected anything except food poisoning at the time?"

"That's right."

"Your uncle continues to give barbecues?"

"Heavens no. He wouldn't go near the barbecue arbor on a bet. Not after what happened there that night. He just closed the gate and put a padlock on it and we've done no more entertaining on cookouts."

"Who was there?" Mason asked.

"All the family. Mildred was there. That was before she knew George Findlay. Then there was my brother Marvin and his wife, Rosemary, and my brother Fowler and his wife, Lolita, who live in the house with Uncle Dee, so they were there. Then Mr. and Mrs. Anson were there, and Uncle Dee, of course, and I think that's all. It was just a family party with the Ansons the only outsiders."

"And this was before George Findlay entered the picture?"

"Oh yes, three or four months before. Mildred hadn't met him at the time."

"Do you remember anything about the evening?"

"Nothing except that it was oppressively warm. We had some drinks at the bar, had dinner and talked a while and then started for the house. It was then that Mr. Anson complained about his stomach. He kept getting worse and his wife decided to take him home. Then Uncle Dee began to have cramps, and pretty quick all of us felt uncomfortable. We got a physician and he asked us what we'd been eating and when we told him about the crab salad, he said he felt certain it was a case of food poisoning, that the crab salad had been in the refrigerator and then had been taken out and that, under those circumstances, bacteria would multiply very rapidly."

"Have the police made any investigation of the barbecue facilities?"

"Oh yes, they were out a week or ten days ago, a couple of plainclothesmen, and Uncle Dee showed them around."

"Did they take photographs?"

"I think they did, yes. And, of course, that man from the insurance company, Herman Bolton, has been there two or three times."

"Why two or three times?" Mason asked. "Wouldn't he have found anything there was to be found and seen it all the first time?"

"I would think so, but he questioned Uncle Dee on two or three occasions, and once he went out to the barbecue arbor and just sat there, looking things over. Then he made a sketch and after that, he took some photographs."

"Well," Mason said, "I'll be on my guard. I don't see how any evidence could be planted at this time, but, of course, there is a point in what you say. If your uncle should be the one who uncovered evidence which had an adverse effect on Selma Anson's case, it would just about break Selma's heart."

"To say nothing of what it would do to Uncle Dee," Daphne said. "I think he'd almost rather kill himself than to go into court with something that would help convict Selma. You think there's going to be a case—a trial, don't you, Mr. Mason?"

"I'm afraid there is," Mason said. "I think the police are working slowly and quietly and have enough of a case to at least go before the Grand Jury and have the Grand Jury return an indictment."

Daphne said, "It's all so terribly cruel and I have a feeling it's all so unjust . . . do you think they stand any chance?"

"What do you mean?"

"Of convicting Selma?"

"Selma Anson," Mason said, "is not a woman who

132

would kill her husband. She's not a woman who would resort to poison. If she didn't poison her husband, and I'm satisfied she didn't, it's going to be very difficult to convict her.

"On the other hand, don't make any mistake about it, Daphne, people have been railroaded to the penitentiary and to the gas chamber by shrewd manipulation of evidence on the part of others."

"You mean it's possible to frame a person for murder?"

"It's very, very possible to frame a person for murder," Mason said.

"You'll see they don't do it to Selma?" she asked. "Please?"

"I'll try my best," Mason promised.

Chapter 16

Paul Drake telephoned at two o'clock in the afternoon.

"Ready for a shock, Perry?"

"Shoot."

"The Grand Jury has indicted Selma Anson for the murder of her husband. I can't tell you how I know, but this is a hot tip right off the wire."

"When did this happen?"

"About twenty minutes ago."

"Thanks a lot, Paul," Mason said. "This gives me a chance to do my stuff."

Mason hung up the phone, said to Della Street, "They've indicted Selma Anson. Get her on the phone just as fast as you can, Della."

Della Street called one number, then, after a moment, shook her head.

"She gave us a second number," Mason said. "Try that."

A moment later Della Street said, "We've caught her at this number. Here she is, Chief."

Mason said, "Mrs. Anson, this is Perry Mason. How fluid are you from a standpoint of cold, hard cash?"

"Why, do you need . . . ?"

"It's not what I need," Mason interrupted. "It's what you're going to need."

"I can raise a considerable sum if I have to."

"A hundred thousand dollars?"

"Yes."

"On half-hour's notice?"

"All I need to do is write two checks."

"Grab your checkbook," Mason said, "and come to the

office just as fast as you can. How long will it take you to get here?"

"About thirty minutes."

"Make it faster than that if you can," Mason said.

The lawyer hung up the telephone, got up and started pacing the floor. After about ten minutes he called Paul Drake.

"Paul," he said, "I want a tail on George Findlay."

"How long a tail?"

"Until I tell you to stop. Take as many men as you have to."

"You know, a real shadowing job runs into money," Drake said. "You'll have to have at least three men working on eight-hour shifts, and you have to give them ten minutes off every couple of hours, and . . ."

"Don't tell me your difficulties," Mason said. "I've got problems of my own. Get a tail on Findlay."

"Will do," Drake said, and hung up.

Mason turned to Della Street. "Get Lieutenant Tragg of Homicide."

She nodded and, after a few moments, said, "He's on the line."

"Hello, Lieutenant," Mason said. "I want to talk with you."

"What about?"

"About murder."

"I'm always willing to talk about murder. Any particular murder?"

"Could be," Mason said. "Will you wait at your office for just a little over thirty minutes?"

"It's important?" Tragg asked.

"It's important," Mason said. "When you hear what I have to say, you'll realize it's quite important."

"I'll be waiting," Tragg promised.

Mason hung up the telephone, and ten minutes later, the phone rang and Gertie said, "Mrs. Anson is in the outer office."

Mason went out to the reception office to greet her.

He escorted her to his private office, closed the door and said, "Mrs. Anson, prepare for a shock. The Grand Jury has indicted you for the murder of your husband."

Her face turned pale. She swayed for a moment, and Della Street, placing an arm around her waist, guided her to a chair.

"Now," Mason said, "I want you to listen and to do *exactly* as I say.

"I'm going to make a big try at getting you out on bail. In order to do that, I have to set the stage very, very carefully."

"I didn't know they allowed bail in murder cases."

"The judge has it in his discretion," Mason said. "Now, I don't know what the evidence is against you. They evidently have something that we don't know about. The gist of our strategy depends on beating the police to the punch. I want you to come with me and I want you to say absolutely nothing unless I am present, and when I am present I want you to leave it to me to do the talking. You will confine all of your answers to simply stating that Mr. Mason will do the talking.

"Now then, I'm going to try to take you down the back way because I have a hunch that it may be a little safer that way."

Mason picked up the phone, said, "Get me the office of the janitor, Gertie." Then said, when he had the janitor's office on the line, "Perry Mason. Can you get the freight elevator up to my floor right away? I have something I want you to take."

"What is it?" the janitor asked suspiciously.

"Twenty dollars," Mason said.

There was a moment's silence, then the janitor said, "Right away, Mr. Mason."

Mason nodded, said to Della Street, "Hold the fort, Della. Remember that Mr. Mason is out. You don't know where he is and you don't know when he'll be back. In the meantime, dash down to the front of the building, get a cab

136

driver, tell him to drive around through the alley and stop at the freight loading entrance of the building."

Della Street nodded.

Mason held the door open for her and Mrs. Anson. Della Street turned to the right and hurried down the corridor to the elevators. Mason, cupping his hand on Mrs. Anson's right elbow, guided her to the left toward the back of the building.

The janitor had the freight elevator waiting, a wide grin on his face.

Mason handed him twenty dollars, which the janitor pocketed with a "Thank you" and a curious appraisal of Selma Anson. The elevator doors closed, the cage rumbled down to the basement.

Mason escorted Mrs. Anson upstairs from the basement to the alley. A cab swung around the corner and into the alley.

Mason signaled the driver. The driver returned the signal, and a moment later, Mason was handing Mrs. Anson into the cab.

"Police Headquarters," he said.

The driver gave Mason a second look, recognized him, said, "Yes, Mr. Mason," and piloted the cab through the alley out into the street and drove deftly to Police Headquarters.

Mason escorted Mrs. Anson into the office of Lieutenant Tragg.

"Lieutenant Tragg," he said, "this is the woman you didn't meet in El Paso. This is Selma Anson."

Tragg fought to keep surprise from his face. "How do you do, Mrs. Anson."

Mason said, "We understand Mrs. Anson has been indicted by the Grand Jury. We're here to surrender and ask that she be booked and taken before the nearest and most accessible magistrate at once."

Tragg said, "Well, this is a job for the D. A."

"All right, then," Mason said, "get the D. A., but I want

137

the record to show that Mrs. Anson has voluntarily surrendered herself."

"How did you know about the indictment?" Tragg asked.

"Wasn't it on the radio?" Mason asked.

"It was *not*!" Tragg said emphatically.

Word passed to the press room that Mason and a woman had entered Tragg's office and newsmen gathered in the corridor.

Tragg sighed, opened the door, and said, "Come on in, boys. This is Perry Mason, the lawyer. He has his client, Selma Anson, with him. She's surrendering on a first-degree murder charge. She's been indicted by the Grand Jury. I'm getting the D. A. on the phone."

"And," Mason said, "we are going to book Mrs. Anson immediately and take her before the nearest and most accessible magistrate."

"As I said, that's a job for the D. A.," Tragg said.

"That," Mason announced firmly, "is a job for the police and the D. A."

Newsmen started shooting flashbulbs, asking questions.

Mason shook his head. "No questions, gentlemen," he said. "Mrs. Anson will make her statement at the proper time, in the proper place, and in the proper manner."

A Deputy District Attorney who was in the building joined the group. Tragg explained to him what was happening.

Mrs. Anson was taken to the women's division of the jail, fingerprinted, booked; then, at Mason's insistence, taken before a committing magistrate.

"If the Court please," Mason said, "I am representing Selma Anson. She has been indicted by the Grand Jury on a charge of first-degree murder. There is not a scintilla of evidence to support the charge and I expect to show that such is the case when the case comes to trial. In the meantime, however, this very refined, very sensitive woman, who has never had any trouble in her life, not even so much as a traffic ticket, finds herself charged with a crime and, despite the shock, she has hurried to the police to sur-

138

render herself and she has come here to place herself on the mercy of the Court."

"What do you mean by that?" the judge asked.

"I feel that this is a case where the defendant should be released on bail."

The Deputy District Attorney said, "Bail is not sanctioned in first-degree murder cases."

"It is in the discretion of the Court," Mason said.

"Here is a woman who has voluntarily surrendered herself. She is willing to put up cash bail in any reasonable amount.

"As the court is well aware, the purpose of bail is not punitive. A person is not adjudged guilty when brought before a committing magistrate for the purpose of fixing bail. The magistrate is only required to inquire into the facts of the case, the circumstances surrounding the defendant, and fix bail, which is solely for the purpose of assuring the State that the defendant will be present at the time of trial.

"In this case the defendant has voluntarily surrendered herself. She is willing to put up a cash bail, not a surety bail, but a bail in cold, hard cash."

"What would you suggest?" the magistrate asked.

"We would be willing to put up fifty thousand dollars as bail."

The Deputy District Attorney was on his feet. "Your Honor, that's ridiculous. This is a first-degree murder case. There is no sum of money which will assure the appearance of a defendant in a first-degree murder case where the death penalty can be asked."

"Is your office going to ask for the death penalty in this case?" Mason asked.

The Deputy District Attorney said, "I don't know. I haven't had an opportunity to confer with my Chief. All I know is that this is an indictment for first-degree murder."

"If you don't know whether you're going to ask for the death penalty," Mason said, "don't try to influence the Court by talking about a first-degree murder penalty."

The judge, who had been studying Selma Anson thoughtfully, said to the Deputy District Attorney, "Do you have any objection to fixing bail on an amount of fifty thousand dollars?"

"I certainly do," the deputy said. "I consider the amount inadequate. I do not think it is a proper case for bail, and . . ."

"The defendant is admitted to cash bail in the sum of one hundred thousand dollars," the judge ruled, "cash or a security bail in an amount of . . ."

"We have the cash right here," Mason said. "Mrs. Anson will write checks and they can be certified within a matter of minutes."

"Very well," the judge ruled, "the defendant is released on bail upon presenting certified checks in the amount of one hundred thousand dollars."

Mason bowed gravely, "Thank you, Your Honor."

Chapter 17

Perry Mason escorted Selma Anson to a seat beside him at the counsel table.

"There's no jury?" she asked.

"There's no jury," Mason said. "We're going to try the case before Judge Leland Crowder."

"But shouldn't we have a jury?"

"It depends," Mason said. "If you are fighting a dead open-and-shut case where the prosecution has everything its own way, you want a jury. You can sometimes play on the sympathies of a jury, or you may convince one or two people out of the twelve jurors and so get a hung jury.

"However, the reason I don't want a jury in this case is because you're out on bail."

"What difference does that make?"

Mason smiled, looked back over the crowded courtroom, glanced at his watch.

"Judge Crowder is a little late. Usually he's the soul of punctuality.

"Crowder is a great one to lock up juries. In cases where there is apt to be any newspaper publicity, the judge would have been almost certain to have locked up the jury for the duration of the trial."

"Well?" she asked.

"Figure the psychological effect," Mason said, "particularly, if some of the people on the jury begin to look at the prosecution's evidence and take it at face value.

"Here's the defendant, accused of murder, walking around free as air, going out to night spots for dinner while the jurors are locked up and herded around like so many cattle.

"They don't like it."

"Yes, I can see your point," Selma Anson said, "but—Mr. Mason, it's terribly important that I remain out on bail."

"I'm going to try to get the judge to continue bail during the trial," Mason said. "I don't know whether we can or not, but . . ."

"Mr. Mason, if the judge convicts me, if I have to go to prison, or even to jail during my trial, I'll die. I'll simply die."

"Oh, it isn't that bad," Mason said, smiling. "At least, your incarceration during the trial would . . ."

"Mr. Mason, I tell you right now, I can't take it. I'm not going to jail."

"You'll have to if the judge tells you to."

"No, I won't. I'll kill myself."

"Are you serious?"

"I'm absolutely deadly serious."

Mason said, "I'm going to do the best for you that I can, but the prosecution has some surprise up its sleeve. I don't know what it is, but they seem to feel it's enough to bring about a conviction."

"What about Judge Crowder, is he fair?"

"Absolutely fair," Mason said. "Moreover, he's open-minded. If he thinks the probabilities are that a person is guilty, but can't say that in his own mind the evidence produces proof beyond a reasonable doubt, he'll turn a defendant loose.

"The prosecutors don't like him. They say . . . Here he comes now."

The bailiff pounded the audience to its feet, intoned the formula bringing Court into session.

Judge Crowder gathered his robe of office around him, seated himself at the bench, nodded to the bailiff.

"Be seated, please," said the bailiff to the audience.

Judge Crowder said, "This is the case of the People of the State of California versus Selma Anson. The defendant is in Court and represented by counsel?"

"Yes, Your Honor," Perry Mason said. "The defendant is here and I represent her."

"The People are ready?" Judge Crowder asked.

Alexander Hilton Drew, a trial deputy who had featured in some rather spectacular trials, and had been highly successful, arose to his feet. "I represent the District Attorney's office," he said.

"Very well," Judge Crowder announced, "proceed."

Selma Anson suddenly whispered to Perry Mason, "That judge looks terribly formidable."

Mason whispered back, "Don't be fooled. He has a ferocious appearance, but he's got a heart as big as all outdoors. And there's one other thing about him."

"What?"

"He's a strong believer in the efficacy of polygraph tests when conducted by a shrewd examiner, and he knows Duncan Monroe and is familiar with his work."

"Oh," Selma said. "I begin to see."

"If the Court please," Alexander Drew said, "since this matter is being tried by the Court without a jury, we will not make any opening statement but will simply let the evidence as it comes in speak for itself."

"Very well," Judge Crowder said. "Call your first witness."

"We call Dr. Boland C. Dawes," Drew said.

While Dr. Dawes was being sworn, Mason said, "We will stipulate the doctor's qualifications, subject to the right of cross-examination."

"Very well," Drew snapped.

The lawyer turned to his witness. "Dr. Dawes, you were familiar with William Harper Anson in his lifetime?"

"I was."

"And you also are acquainted with the defendant, Selma Anson?"

"Yes, sir."

"What relationship existed between Selma Anson and William Anson?"

"Husband and wife."

"William Harper Anson is now dead?"

"Yes."

"Did you treat him during his last illness?"

"Yes."

"Where did he die?"

"In the Nixon Memorial Hospital."

"What was the cause of death?"

"Arsenic poisoning."

"When did you last see the body of William Anson?"

"About twenty-four hours after it was disinterred."

"And did you work with someone else on an autopsy at that time?"

"Yes, sir, I worked with the coroner's autopsy surgeon."

"Do you have any idea how long this poison was ingested prior to death?"

"Judging from the state of the body and the history of the case as I know it, I would say that the poison was ingested about twenty hours before death."

"Do you know where William Anson had been at that period of time—twenty hours before his death?"

"Only by what the patient told me as a history."

"You may inquire," Drew said to Mason.

Mason said to the doctor, "You're quite sure the cause of death was arsenic poisoning?"

"Yes."

"You treated the decedent during his last illness and signed a death certificate?"

"I did."

"And in the death certificate you gave as your opinion the cause of death was a gastro-enteric disturbance, otherwise an acute indigestion."

"I know more now than I did then."

"Answer the question, Doctor. You signed a death certificate listing the cause of death as gastro-enteric disturbance?"

"Yes."

"At that time it didn't occur to you there had been any arsenic poisoning?"

144

"There was no reason why I should have suspected it, no, sir."

"What has caused you to change your mind, Doctor?"

"The analysis we made after disinterment."

"You found arsenic?"

"Yes."

"And because of something the autopsy surgeon for the coroner said to you, you backed up and changed your opinion?"

"Well, we found arsenic."

"Who found arsenic?"

"We both worked on the autopsy."

"Who did the toxicological work?"

"The coroner's office."

"So, you took their word for the presence of arsenic?"

"Yes."

"And promptly proceeded to change your mind as to the cause of death?"

"Oh, all right, if you want it that way, yes. We all of us make mistakes."

"Are you sure you aren't making one now, Doctor?"

"I don't think so."

"But when you made that mistake on signing the cause of death, you were just as positive you were right as you are now?"

"I guess so."

"Thank you, Doctor. That's all."

Drew called Herman J. Bolton to the stand, and showed the insurance policy on the life of William Anson, showed the date of death and the fact that the defendant, Selma Anson, as a surviving widow, had collected one hundred thousand dollars on that insurance policy.

"Did you," Drew asked, "discuss with the defendant, Selma Anson, the circumstances leading up to the cause of death?"

"Yes, sir."

"What did she tell you? Give me her words as nearly as possible."

"She said that she and her husband had been at a barbecue at the house of Delane Arlington, that one of the dishes which had been prepared was a crab salad, that the crab salad had been left out of the refrigerator during a warm afternoon and that she felt sure the crab had become tainted."

"Did she tell you how long that barbecue had been before death?"

"About twenty hours."

"You may cross-examine."

"No questions," Mason said.

"We will call Mrs. Fowler Arlington," Drew said.

Lolita Arlington, looking somewhat sad and dejected, came forward and took the witness stand.

"Your first name is Lolita?" Drew asked.

"Yes, sir."

"I want to get the relationship established here, if the Court please," Drew explained to Judge Crowder.

"Now, your husband is Fowler Arlington?"

"Yes, sir."

"He is the oldest son of Douglas Arlington, who, in turn, is or was a brother to Delane Arlington?"

"Yes."

"And Delane Arlington is your uncle by marriage?"

"Yes."

"You and your husband live in the house with Delane Arlington?"

"Yes, sir."

"It is a big house?"

"A perfectly huge house."

"There is a barbecue grate, a table, chairs, lights and all that goes with an establishment for cookouts in an arbor to the south of the house?"

"Yes."

"I hand you a photograph and ask you if you recognize it."

"Yes, that's a photograph of the arbor."

"And this is a photograph of the Delane Arlington house?"

She studied the photograph. "Yes."

"And this is another view?"

"Yes."

"And a view from still another angle?"

"Yes."

"Your Honor, I would like to have these exhibits introduced in evidence and given appropriate numbers by the clerk."

"No objection," Mason said.

"So ordered," Judge Crowder remarked.

"Now then, were you acquainted with William Anson during his lifetime?"

"I was acquainted with him. I had met him at Uncle Dee's house—when I say Uncle Dee, I mean Delane Arlington, and Uncle Dee invited him to this barbecue, which was sort of a family affair."

"And where did this barbecue take place?"

"In the barbecue arbor."

"Do you remember the time of day?"

"It was about eight o'clock in the evening."

"The lights were on?"

"Oh, yes."

"And you had conversations with the defendant, Selma Anson, from time to time?"

"Oh, yes."

"And you had been trying to draw her out?"

"It depends upon what you mean by drawing her out. I live with my husband in the house of Delane Arlington. I act as his hostess when he gives parties and, as a hostess, I was trying to make Selma Anson feel at home. I was asking her about herself and her hobbies."

"And what did she tell you about her hobbies?"

"She loved to collect specimens of birds. She was a bird watcher, and she had a trap with which she collected specimens without doing damage to the skins."

"You understand she collected birds, that she killed birds?"

"Yes, when she had some specimen she wanted to collect, she did what is known as collecting a bird."

"That means killing a bird?"

"Killing it and skinning it, yes."

"And Selma Anson told you she skinned these birds?"

"Many of them, yes."

"And prepared the skins with a preservative?"

"Yes."

"Did she say what the preservative was?"

"Yes, she told me a trade name. It was called Featherfirm."

"Did she tell you what was in it?"

"She told me, that among other things, it was simply loaded with arsenic, that arsenic was one of the best preservatives she had ever found for keeping bird skins in condition."

"You have heard comment here in Court and elsewhere about a crab salad?"

"Yes, sir."

"Who prepared the crab salad?"

"I did. I may say that Uncle Dee is very, very fond of my crab salad. He likes it made a certain way and, when we have a barbecue, he eats a lot of crab salad. I try to make plenty so there will always be enough."

"And you made the crab salad on this day?"

"Yes."

"This was, by the way, the fifteenth of September?"

"Yes."

"Warm enough to eat out of doors?"

"Oh, yes."

"And you were at that time on daylight saving time?"

"Yes, sir."

"What time did the barbecue take place?"

"We started to eat a little before eight o'clock, daylight saving time."

"Were there refreshments before the barbecue?"

"Oh, yes. We had some drinks and potato chips with a cheese dip."

"And the crab salad was served?"

"Yes."

"How was it served?"

"I was in the kitchen end of the barbecue arbor. I had this huge container of crab salad and I served it on salad plates and Mrs. Anson and Mildred took those dishes and put them at the places at the table where the family was going to sit."

"Were those places labeled?"

"All the family places were. We had a bench and the names of the persons occupying the bench were printed on the wood so that each person had his regular place."

"Now, you say Selma Anson, the defendant, assisted in serving those crab salads?"

"Well, she served some of them. I remember telling her that the really big one was for Uncle Dee because he was very fond of it. And she said that her husband also was very fond of crab salad."

"Do you know that she served the dishes containing the crab salad?"

"I don't know that she served all of them. She may have had some help. I was dishing out the crab salad and getting the French bread ready to be toasted. We wrap it in aluminum foil and put butter inside and—well, I was pretty busy trying to help with the cooking and I can't testify that the defendant served *all* of the salads. But I do remember her taking some of them and serving them, and I very well remember the episode of the dirty dish."

"Will you please tell the Court about what you mean about the episode of the dirty dish?" Drew asked.

"Well, when the barbecue was over and we were clearing off the table, I remember Selma Anson bringing some of the dishes from the table. She started to hand Mildred one dish and said, 'My husband certainly lapped up his salad. He thinks it's the most wonderful crab salad he's ever tasted and'—and then she dropped the dish."

"Dropped it where, to the ground?"

149

"No, there's a brick floor in that part of the barbecue arbor."

"And what happened to the dish?"

"It broke."

"And what happened to the pieces?"

"Selma Anson said, 'Oh, I'm so sorry.' And I said, 'Just drop the pieces in the can here,' and I took the lid off the garbage can which we use for hard garbage."

"There were two cans?"

"Yes, one is used for beer cans and hard garbage, and the other is used for soft garbage."

"Now, what happened to the arbor after that barbecue?"

"Everybody got sick from the crab salad, and, at the time, I blamed myself for it. The refrigerator had been full. I had taken the crab salad out, intending to have Mildred take it down to a second refrigerator we keep in the basement, but both Mildred and I were having our hair done at a beauty shop that afternoon and—well, I just left the crab salad on the kitchen table and we both forgot all about it until after we had got to the beauty parlor."

"Then what?"

"As soon as we came home, we put it back in the refrigerator."

"Now, tell me a little more about what happened with reference to the barbecue arbor. Has it been used recently?"

"After Mr. Anson's death, Uncle Dee was all broken up. He said he didn't care about any more barbecues, nor did he care about entertaining company. He just closed the gate leading to the arbor and we put a lock on it."

"And how long did that lock stay on there?"

"It's there now."

"Who has keys to it?"

"Well, there are keys in the house so that we can get in, but that lock is on the gate all the time so that outsiders can't get in."

"Now then," Drew said, "can you tell us some more about that broken plate which contained the salad which had been eaten by William Anson?"

"Yes, I can. About two weeks ago the police came to me and told me they were investigating the death of William Anson. They asked me what I knew and I told them all about it. Then the man who was in charge, Lieutenant Tragg of Homicide, asked me about the arbor and about what had happened, and asked me if anyone had ever disposed of the garbage after that night.

"I told him the soft garbage had been taken away by the garbage collector, but that the hard garbage usually remained there until the can was full."

"So then what?"

"Then, Lieutenant Tragg asked me to escort him to the arbor. I got the key and opened the gate. He looked into the can of hard garbage and there were some empty beer cans and that broken plate in there."

"The same broken plate?" Drew asked.

"The same broken plate."

"How can you recognize it?"

"I know the plates and the designs and I remember very vividly the pattern in which the plate broke, three pieces."

"And what did Lieutenant Tragg do with reference to that plate?"

"He took it into his possession."

"You don't know what happened to it after that?"

"No, he told me to keep the arbor locked just as it had been and not to let anyone else in and not to talk about the plate."

"And you did as he instructed?"

"Yes."

Drew turned to Perry Mason. "You may inquire."

Mason said, "Did it seem odd to you, Mrs. Arlington, that a very beautiful barbecue arbor be kept locked up simply because some people had had food poisoning and one of them had died?"

"But it wasn't food poisoning," the witness said. "It was a deliberate poisoning."

"So, under the circumstances, it didn't seem odd to you to have the arbor kept locked up?"

"No."

"Then," Mason said, "you must have known for over a year that it wasn't food poisoning."

The witness hesitated, changed positions, then said, "No, I didn't know it until just recently."

"But didn't it seem odd to keep the barbecue arbor locked up?"

"All right," she said, conceding the point. "It was odd. But that was the way Uncle Dee wanted it."

"Thank you," Mason said, "that's all."

Alexander Drew, standing tall, coldly impressive, said, "We will now call Lieutenant Tragg to the stand."

Lieutenant Tragg came forward, carrying a sealed package. He took the oath, seated himself in the witness chair, described his official position, gave his residence, testified as to the length of time he had been on the Homicide Squad, and then was asked by Drew, "Do you know the witness who previously testified, Mrs. Fowler Arlington?"

"I know her."

"Where did you meet her?"

"I met her at the Delane Arlington house—perhaps you should call it a mansion."

"And what happened there?"

"I asked her to show me the arbor where the barbecue had taken place—the one at which William Anson was poisoned."

"And she took you out there?"

"Yes."

"What did you find?"

"I found a locked gate. She had a key to it. I found a complete setup for outdoor cooking. Gas had been piped out to a gas stove on which coffee could be heated. There was an ice-making machine, a portable bar, and, of course, a very elaborate barbecue grate with a table and benches and some folding chairs."

"All protected against the weather?"

"Protected against the weather."

"And what else did you find there, if anything?"

"We opened the garbage can in which Mrs. Arlington said was the hard garbage and we found a broken plate."

"Do you know anything about the history of this plate?"

"Only what I was told by Mrs. Arlington."

"Do you have that plate with you?"

"I do."

"May we see it, please?"

Lieutenant Tragg opened the package, showed a plate broken into three segments.

"Is this in the same condition as it was when you found it?"

"Not exactly the same," Lieutenant Tragg said. "As you can see, it has been processed for fingerprints."

"Did you find any fingerprints on it? Were you able to develop latent fingerprints on that plate so you could tell who had handled it?"

"Yes, sir. The salad dressing had dried into a hard varnish-like substance and latent prints had been perfectly preserved in this dried emulsion."

"Whose fingerprints did you find on it?"

"We found two very fine latent fingerprints which were developed so that a positive identification could be made."

"And what was the identification of the people who had made those prints?"

"The defendant, Selma Anson, was one."

"And the other print?"

"The deceased, William Anson."

"Did you find anything else?"

"We submitted the plate to chemical analysis."

"And what did you find as a result of that?"

"I would prefer to let the toxicologist give his report on that. I was only a witness."

"Did anybody else see the plate or have anything to do with it?"

"Yes, sir, a Mr. Rayburn Hobbs."

"And who is Mr. Rayburn Hobbs, may I ask?"

"Mr. Hobbs is a chemical engineer and also the president of the Hobbs Chemical Company."

"And he saw this plate?"

"Yes, sir."

"And made experiments with it?"

"Yes, sir."

"In your presence?"

"In my presence."

"And can you vouch for the identity of that plate?"

"I can vouch for the identity of this plate as being the one which was recovered from the hard garbage can. It has been in my custody. I have kept it in a sealed package except when it has been taken out for the purposes of experimentation. I have had it under lock in my office."

Drew said, "We ask that this broken plate consisting of three segments be introduced in evidence as the People's Exhibit 5A, 5B, and 5C."

"No objection," Mason said.

"So ordered," Judge Crowder ruled.

"You may inquire," Drew said to Perry Mason.

"Isn't it unusual for a fingerprint to last a long time on a plate of this sort?"

"It is *very* unusual. But in this plate there were very unusual circumstances."

"Such as what?"

"There had been a salad dressing and this salad dressing had been on the fingers of the persons holding the plate when the latent prints were left on the plate. That salad dressing dried, leaving the imprint of the latent fingerprints established on what might be called a permanent basis."

"Did you find the latent fingerprints of two persons?"

"Yes, sir."

"That could be identified?"

"Positively."

"Whose fingerprints were they?"

"A print of the right forefinger of William Anson and of the right thumb of the defendant."

"Any other fingerprints?"

"No others that were identifiable. There were some smudged fingerprints. I may say this, Mr. Mason, that the only fingerprints which were identifiable and the only ones we would expect to have identifiable were the ones that had been made after the fingers had been exposed to this salad dressing and the dressing had dried."

"And do you have any idea how long those fingerprints had been on the plate?"

"They could have been on there for more than a year."

"That isn't what I asked you," Mason said. "Do you have any idea how long those fingerprints had been on the plate?"

"No, sir."

"That salad dressing could have dried in approximately what, twelve hours, twenty-four hours, forty-eight hours?"

"I would say by forty-eight hours it would have been fairly well dried."

"So, for all you know, the prints could have been made on that plate within forty-eight hours of the time you took the plate into your custody?"

"You mean the fingerprints of Selma Anson, the defendant?"

"That's right."

"That," Lieutenant Tragg said, "is correct. The fingerprints of William Anson could hardly have been made on there after his death. Therefore, I consider this established a sort of clock by which we were able to estimate the age of all the prints that we were able to photograph and identify, and I felt that, under the circumstances, the prints must have been made at the time of that barbecue, since Mr. Anson went to the hospital right after the barbecue and died in the hospital."

"Thank you, Lieutenant," Mason said. "No further questions."

Drew said, "I will call Rayburn Hobbs as my next witness."

Hobbs came forward, gave his name and address, qualified himself as a chemical engineer, stated that he was the president of the Hobbs Chemical Company, and had been for some five years.

"And what is the Hobbs Chemical Company? What does it make?" Drew asked.

"It makes a line of chemical preparations, particularly chemical preparations which are used in various hobbies, and we have specialized somewhat on chemicals for taxidermists."

"Are you familiar with a product made by your firm for the purpose of holding feathers on bird skins which are being treated for mounting?"

"I am very familiar with it. I invented the formula."

"That formula has a tradename?"

"Yes, sir."

"What is the tradename?"

"It is called Featherfirm."

"And what is the principal ingredient, or one of the principal ingredients?"

"Arsenic."

"That is of value in treating skins of birds?"

"In the combination in which we have it in this powder it is very effective."

"There are other chemical ingredients?"

"Oh, certainly."

"Now then, I am going to ask you, Mr. Hobbs, if about two years ago you had some trouble with what you considered unfair competition?"

"We did."

"What did you do in connection with that?"

"We had an idea that some of our merchandise was being purchased by wholesalers and sold to retailers who changed the labels on the jars and put it out as a competitive product."

"Could this be done profitably?"

"With certain wholesalers, yes."

"Did you take any steps to remedy that situation?"

"We did."

"What did you do?"

"We put a rather obscure chemical element into certain batches of powder which we sent out."

156

"And what was the purpose of that?"

"We could make an on-the-spot check as to whether this was really our product. I may say that this is done quite frequently by companies that are manufacturing products with a secret formula. A foreign chemical is put in, in exceedingly small quantities, then the powder can be given a spectroscopic analysis and if the lines in the spectroscope show the presence of this foreign element it is readily demonstrable that this product was the product of that manufacturer."

"And you did this with Featherfirm?"

"We did."

"Now then, with reference to this plate which Lieutenant Tragg had introduced in evidence, did you make a spectroscopic analysis of the residue which clung to that plate?"

"We did. We scraped off a dried residue and had it analyzed in a spectroscope and also made a conventional analysis. The dressing which had adhered to the side of that plate contained a large quantity of Featherfirm."

"You may cross-examine," Drew said.

"Are you still putting this element into your compound which you sell under the tradename of Featherfirm?" Mason asked.

"No, sir."

"When did you discontinue it?"

"About six months ago when the competitive situation which we were investigating cleared up. You understand, this element has absolutely nothing to do with the properties of the compound, but is only for the purpose of enabling us to make a speedy identification."

"I understand," Mason said. "I believe that this is a custom of various manufacturers when they wish to be able to trace their product."

"That is right," the witness said. "It's done quite frequently."

"Thank you," Mason said, "I have no further questions on cross-examination."

Drew said, "I'm going to call Thomas Z. Jasper as my next witness."

Jasper, a middle-aged man with a slight stoop, kindly gray eyes and smile lines at the corners of his mouth, took the witness stand, gave his age as fifty-seven and his occupation as conducting a hobby store.

"What sort of hobbies do you refer to?" Drew asked.

"Primarily three hobbies. Rare coins, postage stamps and equipment for amateur taxidermists."

"As a part of your occupation and your experience, are you familiar with a product marketed under the name of Featherfirm?"

"Oh, yes, we sell quite a bit of it. In fact we have the exclusive agency for this city."

"Are you familiar with the personal appearance of the defendant, Selma Anson?"

"Yes, indeed. She has an account, or did have an account at my store."

"Did you ever sell her any of the product known as Featherfirm?"

"Oh, yes."

"How many times?"

"I would say at least half a dozen times."

"Do you know when her husband passed away?"

"Yes. I can't give you the exact date offhand, but I rang her up to express my sympathies."

"Did she ever buy Featherfirm *after* her husband's death?"

"I don't remember that she did. And my books do not indicate that she did. If she did, it was a cash purchase, but my best recollection is that she quit purchasing Featherfirm when she quit buying other taxidermy supplies and this was about the time of her husband's death."

"Thank you," Drew said. "You may cross-examine, Mr. Mason."

"No questions," Mason said.

"If I may have a few moments to consult with Lieutenant Tragg," Drew said, "I think we can perhaps expedite matters. We have been moving along quite rapidly."

158

"I want to congratulate both counsel," Judge Crowder said, "on the fact that this trial is moving along.

"The Court will take a fifteen-minute recess. How many more witnesses do you have, Mr. Prosecutor?"

"We have two or three more. I want to introduce the insurance policy. I want to show the testimony of the toxicologist and the testimony of the autopsy surgeon. I want to show the order for the exhumation of the decedent. I think we can finish today if there's not too much cross-examination. My direct examination will be brief."

"That will be most gratifying," Judge Crowder said. "The Court will take a recess for fifteen minutes."

As the spectators stood silently while Judge Crowder left the courtroom and then turned toward the door, Mason felt a tug at his coat sleeve.

Daphne Arlington said, "Mr. Mason, oh, Mr. Mason, I have to see you at once! It's *terribly* important!"

Mason said to Selma Anson, "You wait right here. Della, you wait with her. See that she doesn't make any statements to the press or to anyone. All right, Daphne, we'll go into this anteroom here. You can talk there."

Mason led the way into the anteroom and Daphne, close to tears, said, "It's happened. And the worst of it is we can't prove it, it's just one of those things."

"Now, come on," Mason said, "get hold of yourself and tell me what it is that's happened."

"They've planted evidence that's deadly and trapped Uncle Dee into finding it."

"How do you know?" Mason asked.

She said, "George Findlay asked Uncle Dee if he had made a really thorough search down there in the arbor, and then he asked Uncle Dee if he didn't think it would be a good plan, under the circumstances, to tear down the arbor and put the barbecue grate at some other place in the yard because of the memory associations. And Uncle Dee agreed and with that idea in mind Uncle Dee went down to look over the place, to make a survey and see what could be done about moving it.

"While he was down there he looked in a cupboard under the sink and, way back in a corner, he saw something. He reached in and took it out and it's a jar half full of Featherfirm.

"Now, you can see what that means. There was absolutely no reason for Selma Anson to bring a jar of Featherfirm over to our place when she was invited out on a barbecue.

"Her defense in the case, of course, is going to be that she was mounting birds and that Featherfirm was a preparation that she needed to preserve the skins and keep the feathers intact.

"But the night of the barbecue her husband was working on a real estate deal and there was absolutely no reason for her to bring any Featherfirm over to the barbecue that night, and certainly no reason for her to secrete it in the back of that cupboard under the sink.

"It's just what I told you. George Findlay and perhaps Mildred, working with him, have planted that bit of evidence. But that, coming on top of all the other evidence, is just going to be too much.

"And they've very skillfully done it so Uncle Dee is the one who has found it and he'll either have to commit a crime concealing evidence, or he's got to take the stand and testify against Selma."

"Tell me," Mason said, "is he in love with Selma?"

"Of course, he's in love with Selma," Daphne said. "I don't think he knew how much he was in love with her at the start, but he's desperately in love with her now and he wants her to marry him. But he knows that she would never think of accepting him now that this cloud is hanging over her head. It's just simply a terrible situation, Mr. Mason."

Mason said, "Sit down, Daphne."

She drew up a chair and sat down at the table.

Mason sat opposite her.

"You think your Uncle Dee is going to go to the authorities and tell them what he has found?"

"He'll *have* to. His conscience wouldn't let him do otherwise, and, of course, if he suppressed evidence he'd be guilty of a crime, wouldn't he?"

"That depends," Mason said.

"Depends upon what?"

"Depends upon the personal relationship of the parties. A husband has a privilege not to be called as a witness against his wife."

"But they aren't married," Daphne said. "Uncle Dee has no wife."

"That's right, he doesn't," Mason agreed.

There were several seconds of silence. Then Mason said, "Pinky Brier is quite a flier. She has a stable of first-class planes, and after all, the defendant, Selma Anson, is out on bail."

Mason abruptly got up from his chair, smiled at the puzzled Daphne, said, "Well, Daphne, I sympathize with your uncle, but, under the circumstances, I can hardly advise him. He has a matter between his conscience and himself."

"Mr. Mason, do you mean if Uncle Dee should . . . ?"

"You're a good egg," Mason interrupted. "You're also intelligent. You have a good pair of ears. You've heard what I said. Under the circumstances, I'd hardly feel that it was proper for me to advise your uncle. Well, I must be getting back into court, Daphne, and see what's happening with my client. I'm afraid the newspaper people will be pestering her for an interview, asking her if she remembers the broken plate, and telling her how the evidence seems to be going against her at this time, and all that kind of stuff that newspaper people are so good at when they want to make a person talk."

Mason walked to the door, turned, smiled at Daphne, who was sitting openmouthed at the table.

"Give Pinky my regards in case you happen to see her," he said, and walked out.

Chapter 18

Judge Crowder returned to court, and the Deputy District Attorney said, "If the Court please, I have one more witness I would like to interrogate this morning before I put the toxicologist on the stand. I have, therefore, asked the toxicologist to be in court at two o'clock this afternoon. Will this meet with the Court's convenience?"

"Probably," Judge Crowder said. "If there is time, however, you can fill in with some other witness. I would like to keep this moving right along."

"Yes, Your Honor. We'll call Mildred Arlington to the stand," Drew said.

Mildred Arlington came marching forward, grim-faced, determined, her lips in a firm, straight line despite the makeup which had tried to convey the impression of a rosebud mouth.

"Your name is Mildred Arlington?" Drew asked.

"Yes, sir."

"What is your relationship to Delane Arlington?"

"I am his niece."

"Do you have any brothers and sisters?"

"No, sir, I am the daughter of Oliver Arlington. I have cousins who are the offspring of Douglas Arlington."

"Where do you live, Miss Arlington?"

"I live in the house with Uncle Dee."

"And were you living in the house with your uncle, Delane Arlington, at the time of the barbecue which preceded the death of William Anson?"

"I was."

"And had been living there for about how long prior to that time?"

162

"About five years."

"You are unmarried?"

"Yes."

"You have a college degree?"

"Yes."

"Who put you through college?"

"Uncle Dee—I mean, Delane Arlington, my uncle."

"Now, do you remember the occasion of the barbecue to which I have referred previously?"

"Yes, sir."

"What were you doing at that barbecue? What was your part in it, your occupation?"

"I was attending the kitchen work and the making of salads."

"Did you make the crab salad?"

"Lolita did."

"Do you remember anything about the salad being served?"

"I do. I was running things very smoothly when Mrs. Anson, that is, the defendant here, insisted on helping.

"I think she meant all right but she was new to the surroundings and didn't know just how to do things, and she kept getting in the way, but we put up with it because we felt her intentions were good."

"And do you remember anything in particular about the crab salad?"

"I remember *very particularly* about the two crab salads which were taken to the two men at the side table."

"When you say the two men at the side table, to whom do you refer?"

"Delane Arlington, my uncle, and William Anson, the deceased husband of the defendant here. They were talking business and so they sat over at one of the little tables which is apart from the long barbecue table where the benches are."

"And what do you remember in connection with those two salads?"

"I put the largest salad on Uncle Dee's plate because

163

when we have a barbecue he is inclined to go rather light on the meat, but when we have the crab salad which either Lolita or I make, he just loves it and makes a meal almost entirely on that.

"I told Mrs. Anson when I handed her the plates, 'This big one is for Uncle Dee and the other one is for your husband.' She nodded and took the plates in her hands and started for the little table.

"I happened to notice, however, that when she got to the end of the long table she pretended that she had spilled some of the salad dressing on her hand and on the plate and she put the two plates down and busied herself with a paper napkin, wiping off the salad plates and wiping her hands. I didn't think anything of it at the time, but she was there for some seconds fussing around over those salad plates."

"Then did you see her serve the salads?"

"No, I didn't. I saw her pick them up again, but I didn't see her at the time she actually served them."

"You have seen the plate that was broken, People's Exhibit Numbers 5A, 5B, and 5C?"

"I have."

"Do you remember anything about it?"

"I remember a great deal about it. I saw Mrs. Anson, the defendant, drop it. It was done deliberately, not accidentally."

"Move to strike that out as a conclusion of the witness," Mason said.

"Motion granted," Judge Crowder said, "but only as to that last part of the answer."

"Cross-examine," Drew said to Mason.

"You helped fix the salad plates yourself?" Mason asked. "That is, you not only prepared the crab salad plates for serving but you served the plates for the two men in question?"

"Yes."

"And your Uncle Dee, as you refer to him, had the largest plate or bowl?"

"Yes."

"You don't like the defendant, do you?"

"No, I do not!" she spat.

"May I ask why?"

"Because I think she is a shrewd, designing woman, and because I am morally certain she murdered her husband."

There was the sound of a collective gasp audible in the courtroom.

"And you would like to see her convicted of that murder?"

"I have no interest in the outcome of this trial. I just don't want that woman in my family. You asked me a question and I have given you a frank answer."

"And when Mrs. Anson returned from serving the salad, did she say anything about having spilled some of the salad dressing?"

"No."

"Did you say anything to her?"

"No."

"Now, later on this salad plate or small bowl that had contained the salad given to Selma Anson's husband became broken?"

"Yes."

"How did that become broken?"

"She dropped it."

"When?"

"When Selma Anson handed it to Lolita, Lolita was busy so I started to take it from the defendant's hand and there was some salad dressing on the outside of the bowl. It was slippery, and she let go of it just before I got my hands on it. She dropped it and it broke."

"And what did you do?"

"We told her we'd just put it in the can for the hard garbage."

"And she did?"

"I did."

"So, the defendant's fingerprint which was found in the dried salad dressing which had adhered to the bowl could have been placed there when she helped pick up the broken dish to put it in the garbage can."

"I don't know when the print was placed there. I didn't see any fingerprint. All I'm telling you is what I know of my own knowledge. I am the one who picked up the broken plate."

"You know that the defendant served the crab salad bowls to the two men at the little table at the west end of the arbor?"

"Yes."

"Thank you," Mason said. "That's all."

Drew said, "If the Court please, I would like to ask an adjournment until two o'clock when I can put my toxicologist on the stand."

"It is approximately eleven-thirty now," Judge Crowder said, and hesitated.

Mason, on his feet, said, "If the Court please, I am going to ask for a recess until tomorrow morning.

"I may state that I think the case can be concluded by tomorrow afternoon. The defense has very little evidence to put on."

Judge Crowder carefully considered the matter. "I have another short case which I *could* take up this afternoon," he said, "if it is agreeable to the prosecutor. What about bail, Mr. Prosecutor?"

"I think that the bail should be canceled at the present time and the defendant held in custody. After all, the Court has seen the dead open-and-shut type of evidence in this case."

Mason said, "The only object of bail is to make the defendant available to court. The defendant not only has put up a hundred thousand dollars in cash, but has extensive property interests in addition."

Judge Crowder was thoughtful. "You will admit, Mr. Mason, that the evidence seems rather convincing at the present time."

"The prosecution's evidence always seems convincing," Mason said.

"Well," Judge Crowder said thoughtfully, "I'll let the bail stand until tomorrow. You think the case can be concluded by tomorrow night, Mr. Mason?"

"If the prosecution rests by noon, we'll have the case in Your Honor's hands for decision by four-thirty. Unless, of course, the prosecutor desires a long argument. As far as the defense is concerned we'll limit our argument to fifteen minutes."

"Under those circumstances," Judge Crowder said, "the Court will adjourn until tomorrow morning at nine-thirty. The defendant is released on her hundred thousand dollar cash bail, which I want all parties to understand will be promptly forfeited in the event the defendant is not here in court tomorrow at nine-thirty."

As court adjourned and the spectators started to file out, Alexander Drew grinned at Perry Mason. "You can see how the judge feels about the evidence," he said, "and I'm not finished."

"Neither am I," Mason told him.

Chapter 19

Perry Mason, Della Street and Paul Drake had lunch at their favorite restaurant reasonably near the Court House.

Drake said, "Don't you think you'd have done better with a jury, Perry?"

Mason shook his head.

"The evidence looks black as your shoe," Drake said. "After all, Bill Anson was poisoned. The only person at that barbecue who could have had any possible motive for poisoning him was his wife, Selma.

"You take that fact, couple it with all of the other facts in the case, and I don't see where Judge Crowder can possibly do anything except find her guilty. After all, Judge Crowder is fair, but you can't sway him by oratory."

"I don't intend to," Mason said. "I'll talk for fifteen minutes and if I can't make a case for my client in fifteen minutes I'll quit trying."

"I'm afraid his mind is pretty well made up right now," Drake said.

"Could be," Mason told him.

Drake looked at him suspiciously. "Perry, are you holding something up your sleeve?"

"My arm," Mason said.

"And what else?"

Mason said, "Oh, maybe a couple of aces. You know the villain in the piece is George Findlay. He's got his eye on a nice little inheritance and he doesn't want to have anything happen which would rock the boat."

"And so?" Drake asked.

"And so," Mason said, "Findlay will be worried that I'm trying to get Selma Anson acquitted. If that happens, he's not entirely certain but what she may become Mrs. Delane Arlington, and when that happens he's pretty certain that his potential inheritance is going to be greatly impaired, or perhaps completely cut off."

"That's quite obvious," Drake said. "I think everybody sees that, that is everybody who has had any contact with the parties."

"The thing to do is to make Judge Crowder see it," Mason said.

"I don't see how you're going to get that brought to Judge Crowder's attention or what particular good it will do if you can get it to his attention," Drake said.

"Findlay," Mason said, "is not one to sit back in idleness. If he thinks there's any chance that the defendant is going to be acquitted he'll try to stack the cards so as to make a conviction doubly sure."

"Well?" Drake asked.

"And," Mason said, "if we could catch him at it, Judge Crowder would take the bit in his teeth and we'd be sitting pretty."

"And you have something up your sleeve?" Drake asked.

"Could be," Mason said laconically. "The best thing we have in our favor is that statement you just made a few moments ago—who could possibly have any motive to murder Bill Anson other than his wife?"

"That statement is in your *favor*!" Drake exclaimed.

"Exactly," Mason said. "It's going to be the whole basis of my argument to Judge Crowder."

Drake stared at Mason in amazement.

The lawyer pushed back his chair, picked up the luncheon check. "Let's go," he said.

After lunch, in the lawyer's office, Mason said to Della Street, "It's two-thirty, Della. Ring up Pinky Brier and see if she's available."

"Are we going somewhere?"

"*We* aren't," Mason said. "But I'd like to see if she's available. Just ask where she is. Tell whoever answers the phone that it's not particularly important, but we're just trying to keep a line on her."

Della Street put through the call, talked for a moment, then turned to Perry Mason. "Pinky," she said, "left for Las Vegas, Nevada, about an hour ago. She had two passengers, a man and a woman. Does that mean anything to us?"

Mason said, "Does it suggest anything to you, Della?"

Della Street regarded the lawyer with wide-eyed admiration. "You clever so-and-so of a such-and-such!" she said.

Chapter 20

At nine-thirty, when Judge Crowder had taken his place on the bench, and the audience had been seated, Hamilton Burger, the District Attorney, came marching into court and took his seat beside Alexander Drew.

Judge Crowder regarded the addition to the prosecutor's staff with apparent surprise.

"You have a separate matter to take up with the Court, Mr. District Attorney?"

"No, Your Honor," Hamilton Burger said, "a matter has arisen in this case which is so important that I desire to present it in person."

"Go ahead," Judge Crowder said.

"If the Court please," Hamilton Burger said, getting to his feet with ponderous dignity, "it has come to my attention that very important new evidence has been discovered in this case; that in some manner the defense attorney, Perry Mason, learned of this discovery before the police did, and I believe that Perry Mason has been taking steps to obstruct the introduction of this evidence."

"That is a very serious charge," Judge Crowder said.

"The prosecution is in a position to prove it!" Hamilton Burger snapped.

"Would you care to make a formal statement?" Judge Crowder asked.

"The facts are simply these, Your Honor. We have reason to believe that Delane Arlington found a very important piece of evidence which had heretofore been overlooked; that he consulted with his niece, Daphne, about this evidence; that Daphne, in turn, went to Perry Mason; that Perry Mason arranged to have the witness, Delane Arlington, take a plane and leave the jurisdiction of the court, going to another state, returning only this morning, and refusing to discuss any aspect of the case or the nature of his evidence with officers.

"The police are, therefore, baffled to find out the details concerning this evidence, except they know generally and from hearsay evidence that a jar of the arsenic compound marketed under the tradename of Featherfirm was found in the back part of a cupboard at the scene of the fatal barbecue.

"Since there was no reason on earth for any preparation used in the preservation of bird skins to be present at the site of this barbecue, but since there was every reason on earth for a poisoner to have this preparation there, this becomes a very damning piece of evidence and we feel that the process of the Court is being abused by any runaround which keeps us from having this jar in our possession."

"Do you know where this piece of evidence is at the present time?" Judge Crowder asked.

"I want to interrupt these proceedings long enough to find out," Hamilton Burger said. "I want to call witnesses to the stand, and I am asking the Court that, under the circumstances, the bail of the defendant be canceled and the defendant remanded to custody."

Judge Crowder frowned down at Perry Mason. "Mr. Mason," he said, "do you care to answer these charges?"

"No, Your Honor, all I request is that the Court reserve its ruling on the question of bail until all the evidence is before the Court."

Judge Crowder shook his head. "I have been uneasy about this case ever since yesterday morning. I think it is a case where the defendant should be incarcerated. The Court is going to cancel the order admitting this defendant to bail, and this defendant is remanded to custody.

"Now then, Mr. Burger, if you have any evidence you want to put on, go ahead."

"I want to call Daphne Arlington," Burger said.

Daphne Arlington took the witness stand, gave her name, her address, her relationship to Delane Arlington.

"Did your uncle come to you yesterday and tell you that he had uncovered something in the barbecue arbor which caused him a great deal of worry?" Hamilton Burger asked.

"Objected to on the ground it calls for hearsay evidence," Mason said.

Hamilton Burger frowned. "I am not asking for the evidence at the present time. I am simply trying to get at a conversation which will pave the way for calling Delane Arlington to the stand."

"I still object on the ground that it's hearsay. If he wants to ask the witness if Delane Arlington made any statement about having evidence in his possession, he should first call Delane Arlington, and then use this witness as an impeaching witness."

"Is there any objection to calling Delane Arlington?" Judge Crowder asked.

"I would prefer to lay the foundation first," Hamilton Burger said, "but if the Court wants it done that way, we'll do it that way. You are excused, Miss Arlington, and I will call Delane Arlington to the stand."

Arlington came forward and took the witness stand.

"Your name is Delane Arlington? You are the owner of the house where the barbecue which has been under discussion in this case took place?"

"Just a moment," Mason said. "May I ask the prosecution if the purpose of this question is to build up a case against Selma Anson, the defendant, in this case?"

"It certainly is," Hamilton Burger snapped.

"Then," Mason said, "I would like to point out that this witness has a privilege not to be called."

"What do you mean, a privilege not to be called?" Judge Crowder snapped.

"He is the husband of the defendant," Mason said.

For a long moment there was shocked silence in the courtroom. Then Hamilton Burger, his face purpled, shouted at Perry Mason, "So, *that's* why you insisted on having your client out on bail. That's why you took advantage of the process of the Court to obstruct the administration of justice!"

Judge Crowder tapped emphatically with his pencil. "Let me handle this, Mr. Prosecutor," he said.

"If I may make one statement first," Perry Mason said, "I think it will clarify the situation."

Judge Crowder said, "I am not entirely certain that I care to have your statement at this time, particularly in view of the fact that the Court does not like the situation which is being disclosed. To take advantage of the fact that a defendant is out on bail to have her marry one of the witnesses for the prosecution is, to my mind, perverting the ends of justice. I intend to look into this very carefully, both from the standpoint of ethical practice, and also from a standpoint of taking advantage of the Court. Now then, if you wish to make any statement in view of those facts, you are at liberty to do so."

"I wish to make a statement," Mason said. "I wish to state that the marriage of Delane Arlington and Selma Anson was not for the purpose of obstructing the administration of justice. They had been going together for some time, in fact I think if it hadn't been for Arlington's interest in the defendant this case might never have been brought to trial. Now then, in order to show my good faith, I am going to state that it is my understanding of the present law that the witness has a privilege not to testify, but I will advise the witness, on behalf of the defendant, not to claim that privilege. We will ask that the witness be permitted to testify. I simply want the Court to understand that this is being done voluntarily on the part of the defendant and her husband, and that this is the best answer to the District Attorney's contention that the marriage was for the purpose of obstructing the interests of justice. The marriage was the culmination of a romantic interest between the parties.

"In short," Mason said, "to spare this witness any embarrassment, and, at the same time, to place all of my assistance at the service of the District Attorney in order to ferret out

174

the real truth in the case, I will stipulate that yesterday morning the witness went to the arbor where the barbecue took place and in checking around in a dark corner of the cupboard below the sink at the kitchen end of the arbor he found a jar of Featherfirm, the jar being about half empty.

"I will further stipulate that the witness, tremendously embarrassed and emotionally upset because of this finding, turned the jar over to his niece, Daphne, who, in turn, gave it to me.

"I have this partially empty jar with me in court, and it gives me great pleasure to offer to introduce it in evidence, if I may do so, as a Defendant's Exhibit."

"A *Defendant*'s Exhibit!" Hamilton Burger shouted.

"Exactly," Mason said, "a Defendant's Exhibit."

Delane Arlington, on the stand, stared in openmouthed amazement at the lawyer.

Mason produced a jar of white powder and approached the witness. "This is the jar of white powder which you gave to Daphne?"

"Just a moment," Hamilton Burger interposed. "I'll take the stipulation of the defendant rather than risk technical error by having the husband of the defendant—and I will take the word of the Counsel for the defense that he is the husband—be instrumental in presenting any evidence which would result in her conviction."

"This is a *most* unusual situation," Judge Crowder said.

"Very well," Mason said, "I will now try to introduce this as the Defendant's Exhibit.

"I further wish to state to the Court that the marriage of Delane Arlington and the defendant was the result of a romantic attachment.

"As the Court will presently observe there is not only no reason for the defendant to try to prevent the introduction of this piece of evidence, but it is very much in her favor to have it introduced.

"In order to identify this as evidence for the defense, I wish to interrogate some witnesses on their *voir dire*.

"I will first ask Lieutenant Tragg to come forward."

Tragg took his position on the witness stand amid a breathless silence of intense interest.

"A short time ago you searched the arbor where the barbecue was held at the time the defendant's husband ingested poison, or at the time it was claimed he had ingested poison, and found the broken plate which you have introduced in evidence?"

"Yes, sir."

"At the time you made that search, did you search *all* of the arbor?"

"Yes, sir."

"Is there any possibility, any possibility at all, that, during such search, you could have overlooked a jar of Featherfirm such as I now hand you which could have been in a dark corner of the cupboard compartment underneath the sink in the kitchen area of that arbor?"

"Just a minute!" Hamilton Burger said. "I object to this evidence being handled by the defendant's lawyer and being in the custody of the defendant. This is the prosecution's evidence, and heaven knows how many fingerprints have been eradicated by reason of the handling of this piece of evidence."

"It's a piece of *defendant*'s evidence," Mason said. "The defense certainly doesn't have to turn all of *its* evidence over to the prosecution as soon as the defense finds the evidence."

"Now, just a minute, just a minute," Judge Crowder said. "There's a question which has been asked the witness. Let's hear what the witness has to say in answer to that question."

"Very well," Mason said, "answer the question, Lieutenant. Could you have overlooked this piece of evidence?"

"Absolutely not!" Lieutenant Tragg said. "This is the first I had heard about any such evidence being discovered, but I will state that we searched every inch of that arbor. As far as the cupboard beneath the sink is concerned and the so-called dark corner, there weren't any dark corners to a police search. I had a powerful flashlight and I examined every nook and cranny of that cupboard."

"Thank you," Mason said. "That's all."

"Do you have any cross-examination?" Judge Crowder asked Hamilton Burger.

"No," the flabbergasted Hamilton Burger said. "Not for the moment."

Mason said, "I now wish to call Rayburn Hobbs to the stand."

Hobbs, who was in court, came forward and took his position in the witness box.

"I show you a jar purporting to contain Featherfirm," Mason said, "and ask if you have seen that before."

"I have."

"When?"

"Early this morning."

"What did you do?"

"I marked my initials on the jar, that is, I etched them so that I could identify the jar. I analyzed the contents under a spectroscopic analysis to see if there was present any of the identifying chemical which had been used in order to identify our product."

"Did you find any such chemical?"

"No."

"And what does that indicate?"

"It indicates that this product was manufactured by us and sold within the last six months. Moreover, the label is from a fresh batch of labels which we had printed which are almost identical with the older labels but have a small key number in the upper right-hand corner and this indicates that the label was put on that jar within the last three months because we didn't have these labels prior to that time."

"Cross-examine," Mason said to the District Attorney.

Hamilton Burger hesitated a moment, then said, "You're absolutely certain, Mr. Hobbs?"

"Positive," Hobbs said.

Hamilton Burger sat down.

"That's all."

"Call Thomas Z. Jasper," Mason said.

Jasper took the stand in a breathless silence. A faint smile twitched the corners of Judge Crowder's mouth.

"Now then," Mason said, "I want you to look around the courtroom and see if you recognize any customers in the courtroom . . . No, no, now, just a moment, please. Mildred Arlington, I am going to ask you to stay, and George Findlay, please resume your seats. Don't leave the courtroom."

Jasper said, "Those two people are familiar to me, Mr. Mason."

"Where did you meet them?"

"The young woman came into my place about fourteen months ago and wanted some Featherfirm."

"You remembered her all this time?"

"I remembered her because of the impression she made. She quite evidently knew nothing about taxidermy. She wanted Featherfirm. I asked if she was buying it for a friend. She said she was buying it for herself."

"And the gentleman who is standing as if ready to make a run for it?"

"That gentleman was in my store about a week ago and purchased a jar of Featherfirm."

Mason said, "Would you care to cross-examine, Mr. Burger?"

Burger, looking from the witness to George Findlay, who had slowly seated himself, and to Mildred Arlington, who sat straight and defiant, said, "No, no questions."

"Now, then," Mason said, "I want to recall Delane Arlington."

"As *your* witness," Hamilton Burger said.

"As my witness," Mason said.

Delane Arlington, looking thoroughly confused, took the witness stand.

"Mr. Arlington," Mason said, "you were exceedingly fond of the crab salad made by your niece, Mildred."

"Yes."

"You pretty well filled up on crab salad whenever you had a barbecue and either Lolita or Mildred made the salad, did you not?"

"That's right."

"Now," Mason said, "I want you to think carefully. Think back to the time of the meal when William Anson is supposed to have ingested the poison. Do you remember Selma Anson serving two crab salads at the table where you were sitting with William Anson?"

"Yes, I do. I remember that very distinctly. I . . . If you want me to answer these questions frankly, I'll answer them frankly. I remember she served the salads."

"Now, then," Mason said, "is there any possibility, and I want you to think carefully before you answer, that you said to William Anson, 'I have a bigger dish of salad than you do. Let's change if you like the salad'?"

The witness frowned thoughtfully, then suddenly his face lit up, "Good heavens, yes!" he said. "That's *exactly* what happened. I remember Anson telling me that he loved crab salad. That it was his favorite dish, and I told him, 'Here, I have a bigger dish than you. Take mine.'"

"And you swapped dishes?"

"We swapped dishes."

"Thereby," Mason said, "saving your life.

"I now wish to introduce this planted jar of Featherfirm as evidence as part of the defendant's case, showing that not only was an attempt made to frame this defendant on a charge of murder, but that the poisoning of William Anson was accidental. The dose of fatal poison was intended for Delane Arlington.

"There was only one person who would have had any motive for poisoning William Anson and that was the defendant, Selma. But there were several persons who would have had a motive for poisoning Delane Arlington, and one of those persons was his rather acrimonious niece, Mildred."

Mason turned to Hamilton Burger. "Do you have any questions of this witness?"

Hamilton Burger, engaged in a whispered discussion with his trial deputy, said, "No questions."

"Now then," Mason said, "if the prosecution will rest its case, the defense will submit its case without argument."

Hamilton Burger said, with poor grace, "The prosecution rests."

"The defense rests," Mason said, "and submits the case without argument."

"Do you care to argue?" Judge Crowder asked Hamilton Burger.

"Not *this* case," Hamilton Burger said disgustedly.

Judge Crowder said, "The Court finds the defendant not guilty. She is released from custody. Her bail is exonerated. The Court further directs that Mildred Arlington and George Findlay be taken into custody pending a further investigation.

"The Court will make this order on the ground of tampering with evidence before the Court, and they will be ordered to show cause why they shouldn't be sentenced for contempt of court and the fabrication of evidence.

"The Court would suggest to the prosecution, however, that these two be taken into custody for murder as principal and accessory after the fact.

"Court is adjourned."

The judge arose and started for his chambers.

The spectators burst into uproarious applause.

Judge Crowder turned and started back to the bench as though intending to suppress the demonstration; then, looking down at Selma and Delane Arlington, wrapped in each other's arms, the jurist smiled and continued on his way into chambers.

Mason, gathering up his briefcase and his papers, virtually smothered with congratulations from the spectators, caught the eye of George Findlay.

Mason made him a little bow. "Cupid," he said, "a somewhat cavalier cupid, very much a contraband and a very careless cupid, but cupid, nevertheless. You brought about a marriage. Good morning, Cupid."

George Findlay, with a bellow of rage, pushed past the spectators to take a swing at Mason, but his arm was grabbed from behind by a Deputy Sheriff, who said, "None of that, buddy. Take it easy. You're in custody."

Perry Mason mysteries by
ERLE STANLEY GARDNER

Call toll free 1-800-793-BOOK to order by phone and use your major credit card. Or use this coupon to order by mail.

__THE CASE OF THE AMOROUS AUNT	345-37878-4	$4.50
__THE CASE OF THE ANGRY MOURNER	345-37870-9	$4.50
__THE CASE OF THE BLONDE BONANZA	345-37877-6	$4.50
__THE CASE OF THE BORROWED BRUNETTE	345-34374-3	$4.99
__THE CASE OF THE CALENDAR GIRL	345-34375-1	$4.99
__THE CASE OF THE CARELESS CUPID	345-39226-4	$4.99
__THE CASE OF THE CARELESS KITTEN	345-36223-3	$4.99
__THE CASE OF THE CAUTIOUS COQUETTE	345-35202-5	$3.99
__THE CASE OF THE DARING DECOY	345-36220-9	$4.99
__THE CASE OF THE DROWNING DUCK	345-37868-7	$4.50
__THE CASE OF THE DROWSY MOSQUITO	345-37869-5	$4.99
__THE CASE OF THE FAN-DANCER'S HORSE	345-37144-5	$3.99
__THE CASE OF THE FENCED-IN WOMAN	345-39223-X	$4.99
__THE CASE OF THE FUGITIVE NURSE	345-37873-3	$4.50
__THE CASE OF THE GREEN-EYED SISTER	345-37872-5	$4.50
__THE CASE OF THE HALF-WAKENED WIFE	345-37147-X	$4.99
__THE CASE OF THE HESITANT HOSTESS	345-37871-7	$4.50
__THE CASE OF THE HORRIFIED HEIRS	345-39227-2	$4.99
__THE CASE OF THE LONG-LEGGED MODELS	345-37876-8	$4.99
__THE CASE OF THE LUCKY LOSER	345-36497-X	$4.99
__THE CASE OF THE NERVOUS ACCOMPLICE	345-37874-1	$3.99
__THE CASE OF THE ONE-EYED WITNESS	345-39225-6	$4.99
__THE CASE OF THE QUEENLY CONTESTANT	345-37879-2	$4.50
__THE CASE OF THE RUNAWAY CORPSE	345-36498-8	$4.99
__THE CASE OF THE SCREAMING WOMAN	345-37875-X	$4.99
__THE CASE OF THE SINGING SKIRT	345-37149-6	$3.99
__THE CASE OF THE STUTTERING BISHOP	345-35680-2	$3.99
__THE CASE OF THE SULKY GIRL	345-37145-3	$4.99
__THE CASE OF THE TROUBLED TRUSTEE	345-39224-8	$4.99

Name_____
Address_____
City_____ State_____ Zip _____

Please send me the BALLANTINE BOOKS I have checked above.
I am enclosing $_____
  plus
Postage & handling* $_____
Sales tax (where applicable) $_____
Total amount enclosed $_____

*Add $4 for the first book and $1 for each additional book.

Send check or money order (no cash or CODs) to:
Ballantine Mail Sales, 400 Hahn Road, Westminster, MD 21157.

Prices and numbers subject to change without notice.
Valid in the U.S. only.
All orders subject to availability.   GARDNER

Coming soon to
your local bookstore!

Perry Mason

in

THE CASE OF THE HORRIFIED HEIRS

and

THE CASE OF THE POSTPONED MURDER

by

ERLE STANLEY GARDNER

Published by Ballantine Books.